How To Confuse A.I.

How To Confuse A.I.

Peter Wick

Azzurri Publishing

How to Confuse A.I.

by

Peter Wick

Also by Peter Wick:

Movies

Long Strange Trip (or, the Writer, The Naked Girl, and The Guy With a Hole in His Head) – *(1999 - Amazon)*

Movie Pizza Love – *(2008 -Youtube)*

Rock Paper Scissors – *(2011 – Amazon)*

Silk Finds What He's Looking For (documentary) – *(2021 - Youtube and IMDb)*

Books

(World-wide paperback and amazon Kindle)

Key West – original novel (2013)

Key West – Special Edition (2015)

Key West – the Companion Episodes (2015)

It Is What It Is – (2015)

Funny Sexy Nanobots (and other improvements) – 2017)

The Past is Going to Suck (A time-traveler's guide to the 20th century) – (2018)

Milo and Meg are Solid – (2020)

Forward, prologue, apologies and disclaimers:

This book, more than anything else I've written, is full of references to other things; books, movies, well...those two things mostly, books and movies. I am listing here many of these referenced works, just to be open and up front about it, since you'll probably recognize some of them as you read. I did it on purpose. So...here is a list of some, many, most of the previous works that I directly refence in How To Confuse A.I. This list may or may not be complete. Here we go; The Hitchhiker's Guide to The Galaxy, by Douglas Adams, The Stanley Kubrick films Dr. Strangelove and 2001: A Space Odyssey, Catch 22 (both the book and the 1969 film, and I suppose also George Clooney's mini-series), Blade Runner, 1984, Brave New World, The Terry Gilliam film Brazil, The Trial by Franz Kafka (and the Orson Welles film adaptation), Minority Report (and by definition, some of these films suggest that I am also referencing a lot of writing by Phillip K. Dick), Being John Malkovich, Eternal Sunshine of The Spotless Mind, A.I. Artificial Intelligence by Stephen Spielberg (and sort of Kubrick), Natural Born Killers, and I suppose, to a degree, Monty Python's Life of Brian.

Is that a complete list?

Good question.

-Peter Wick

Prologue

The Dawn of Humanity

Kag squatted in front of the cave wall.

He dipped the point of his stick in the bowl of red berry pigment and lifted it toward the wall.

He stroked the red pigment to his right, painting the direction of an arrow flying toward a deer.

He had not painted the deer yet.

This was all Kag cared about, this painting.

"Kag!"

His older brothers Nog and Gog stood impatiently behind him.

"Kag, come on. We have hunting and gathering to do. The sun's already been up for an hour."

Kag did not respond. He peered intently at his cave wall painting. He moved his hand carefully toward the painting. With his stick he added a tiny dab of pigment to the tip of the arrow.

"Kag!"

Satisfied with his revision of the arrow, Kag finally responded without turning around.

"What's that?" Kag asked sarcastically. "Another day of hunting and gathering? Ooh! So exciting! I'm tingly with excitement. How will this day of hunting and gathering be different from –" Kag finally stood and faced his brothers, "the other freaking five thousand days we've spent hunting and gathering?"

"Oh, don't go off on that again." Nog looked at Gog and rolled his eyes.

"There's got to be something better than this," Kag complained, his brothers were certain, for the millionth time. "I dream of a time when we have machines in our homes that keep our food cold until we pull it out and cook it."

"Machines!" Nog said mockingly. "What the hell are machines?"

"And what is a home?" asked Gog, laughing.

"It's where we live." Kag shifted his feet, frustrated with his brothers. "You don't think humanity is going to live in caves forever, do you?"

Nog rolled his eyes again. "Someone's going to live in the looney bin if he's not careful."

Nog and Gog laughed together. Then Gog stopped. "Hey, what's a looney bin?" he asked.

Kag interrupted once again. "There has to be more to life than this, all the hunting and the gathering."

"Look, mate," Nog replied sharply, "you're living in a fantasy world. Hunting and gathering is all there is and all there ever will be."

Kag knew he would never convince his brothers. Reluctantly he joined them, and the three brothers began walking out of the cave opening.

"Well, do we have to do both?" Kag asked weakly. "Do we have to hunt AND gather? Isn't gathering enough for one person? I have to hunt also?"

2075 – The Lunchtime of Humanity

One

Down is up

It wasn't really Adam's fault that everything collapsed.

It wasn't really Amy's fault either.

They were just trying to live their lives, trying to make sense of the chaos.

There was one flaw in the system, it turned out, and that one flaw just happened to work in their favor.

It didn't seem to be working for them at first. It didn't appear to be working in their favor for quite some time.

***

Los Angeles bustled with activity.

People - both real and simulated – carried out their busy day, getting into pods, going to work, to school, shopping. Many of them bustled about remotely – projecting themselves onto the streets from the comfort of their own homes. Others, like Adam Douglas, actually moved about the city in person.

Looking down from above – as so many of the drones operated by the Antarctica Corporation were doing – it looked like another normal day in the life of the city.

Adam stood on the sidewalk in the middle of the block. He reached his hand to the back of his neck where his Life-Lynq chip was implanted, tried to adjust it slightly, and stepped off the sidewalk into the nearly empty street.

Halfway across the street a sharp irritation shot into his neck from the chip. He looked up and saw his picture – larger than life – flashed on the side of the large building in front of him.

"Jaywalking!" the messaged screamed. "Social score down 3 points!"

Adam's face flushed with embarrassment. Mothers grabbed their children and hurried them away. Everyone on both sides of the street shook their heads and turned away.

Adam ducked inside the building as quickly as he could.

The news came up everywhere. It was impossible to avoid. It simply appeared.

"Tyrell Elon Zuzerzos, Founder and CEO of the Antarctica Corporation, is celebrating the five-year anniversary of purchasing the United States of America. The year was 2070, and U.S. debt had gotten so out of control that the unthinkable was suddenly thinkable. Zuzerzos stepped up and made an incredible offer. He bought all U.S. debt, he bought the whole country, and privatized the government. And now, here with a word to celebrate our fifth anniversary, Tyrell Elon Zuzerzos."

Zuzerzos' face appeared live. He smiled a slick smile, beaming out at the nation with confidence. "I can't even begin to tell you how proud I am of all of you. In these challenging times, you, the customers - I mean citizens - of America, have stepped up and handled adversity so amazingly well. Congratulations America!"

He smiled an even bigger smile and continued. "Never forget that down is up, America. Never forget! If you can just BELIEVE it, anything is possible! You just have to believe, America! We have faced so many challenges. Because of the Bio-Wars, and the lingering viruses and diseases from those wars, we have had to make tough decisions and life-style adjustments. The biggest, as you all know, is that due to these lingering viruses, human-to-human relationships have sadly been banned."

Zuzerzos paused. He looked out at the nation.

"But we are a nation of great minds and innovators!" he continued. "We at Antarctica Corp have given you the Simu-Network; the most advanced, flawless simulated human and intelligence network ever developed. The Simu-Network has never made a mistake. It is the most perfect human and intelligence simulation ever created. You're welcome, America! Stay strong, America. The Bio-Wars are nearly over, but we all must stay vigilant. We in the Western World must keep our guard up. The Others are still out there. The Others are still dangerous! Stay strong, America. Stay strong, and soon we can celebrate! Celebrate! Down is up, America! DOWN IS UP! Anything is possible!"

And Zuzerzos disappeared from the screen as wild cheers rose up, seemingly from everywhere. Adam looked around and did not see anyone cheering, yet the sound was overwhelming and deafening. He turned back to the news as the disclaimer ran, too fast for most to see or even notice; "The United States of America is a wholly-owned subsidiary of the Antarctica Corporation."

***

Adam walked slowly down the hallway. Adam was real. The lines in his fifty-something face gave him away. The gray sprinkled though his blond hair gave him an unusual look, a natural human look, a look that was becoming more and more unacceptable with each passing year.

He stopped for a moment and reached his hand to the back of his neck. He touched the Life-Lynq chip – this damn neck-chip! – and wished he could remove it. He continued walking.

He flipped his eyes to the right and was annoyed with the ad that popped up.

"Where do you want to visit?" the ad asked in a chirpy voice. "Italy? Mozambique? The town where you grew up? Just kidding, who would want to visit the town where they grew up?

"Travel Cheetah has you covered."

Glossy and inviting images danced around Adam. He tried to wait them out to get to the news clip.

"Reasonable prices, more destinations than you can imagine." The voice was cheery and perky, but with just a hint of sarcasm.

"Visit sunny Cancun on your lunch break. Stay for a week, or stay forever under an assumed name after robbing a bank.

"Sorry, that's against the law, and you'd be found out anyway."

"Adam!" It was Amy's voice from behind him down the hallway.

"Hey, Amy," Adam responded, a happy smile forming on his face. "Amy, why do I always get your ads? Travel Cheetah, I mean, I hardly ever travel."

Amy was also real, but she was better at it than Adam. Well into her 40's, Amy maintained that beautiful ageless professional look. She was charming and had a spark in her eye. It was a spark full of devastating sarcasm, but a spark that nearly always exuded simple charm.

Amy had made her way to Adam, and with a comfortable familiarity born of several years as co-workers, they walked together out the large double doors – which opened for them. Adam wondered why the doors always opened with a very subtle sigh of satisfaction. They found themselves outside.

"It's a sign, Adam. You need a vacation."

"Is it that obvious?"

"Let's just say I can tell your new campaign is weighing you down. How's it coming along?"

"It's good. It's basically d –"

They were interrupted by a co-worker walking up behind them. "Adam, Amy. Hey friends, what's up?"

Amy looked around and pulled off a masterful performance of a pleasant and happy co-worker. "Hey, Jeremy," she said.

"We should all hang out together sometime," Jeremy said, his not-quite human awkwardness creeping into the conversation ever so subtly.

Adam froze in silent horror. Amy took over.

"Hey, Jeremy," she began with a smile, "What's the name of that guy, you know, the guy who, the one whose name isn't Bill?"

"Hm," Jeremy was suddenly stumped. "There are many people not named Bill. Do you mean Ted? Here are some other names that are not Bill; Steve –"

"No, not that one, the other one," Amy said, the sarcasm barely detectable.

Jeremy looked down and pondered the riddle. "There are so many people with so many names. I don't know which ones are relevant." He looked back at Amy. "Can you possibly refine your search?"

"Not right now, Jeremy," Amy said, sounding empathetic and supportive. "Tell you what, Jeremy, you go home and sort through your results tonight, and get back to me tomorrow."

"Okay....okay, yeah I will," Jeremy said. He turned around and walked back into the building, his head down in thoughtful contemplation.

Amy and Adam looked at each other and shared a smile.

"How do you do it, Amy?"

"How do I do what? I don't know what you're talking about."

But Amy's smile assured Adam that she knew exactly what he was talking about.

"Hey!" Amy blurted out, almost startling Adam. "Brad and I are having a wingding this weekend. Why don't you and Trilda come? Saturday night, six o'clock."

Adam had stopped paying attention. He was watching three children run out of the building, screaming happily together, as they raced toward a waiting pod and got in.

"Adam?"

"Hm?"

Amy looked Adam in the eye.

"Oh, sorry," Adam said, shaking his head. "Hey, why do

they include Simu-children? What's the point of that? And why do they have them here at Corporate Day Care?"

"I don't know. Maybe to help orient the real kids to their Simu friends? I mean, even the real kids are made in a test tube. It's not like when we grew up and Moms and Dads actually made their kids during a moment of passion."

Adam shook his head. "Anyway, sorry, what were you saying?"

"Saturday, six o'clock. You and Trilda come over to our weekend wingding."

Adam smiled back at her. "Okay, uh, sure, sure."

Amy brushed some lint off of Adam's shoulder. "You don't exactly sound enthusiastic, Adam," she mused.

Adam looked back at her. "God, Amy, sometimes I wonder where my life went."

"You're living your life, Adam."

"I wanted to be creative, you know, CREATIVE. But all I do is make these stupid ads."

"You are creative, Adam," Amy said.

"How did we end up like this?" Adam was looking absently into the distance. "How did these bio-wars turn into this? Fake relationships, neck chips?"

Amy kept her reassuring smile. "So…Saturday? Six o'clock? You and Trilda?"

"Oh, sure, I guess."

"You guess?"

"I don't really want to talk about it, you know, out loud."

"Are you going to make me read your mind, Adam? You know only Antarctica can do that."

"I – I've been having some issues with – with – "

"With Trilda?" Amy asked.

"How long has it been, Amy?" Adam asked absently. "I mean, you remember real relationships."

"Adam, what are you talking about? Shut up. Nothing's more real than the Simu-Network." Then she added, in a perfect impression of the advertising, "The most advanced algorithm ever developed."

"You sound like a commercial."

"Of course I do, Adam. We work in advertising."

Adam looked blankly to his left and right. He looked at Amy and nodded.

"Just take her into the shop. Have a diagnostic done. I took Brad in a couple weeks ago. She'll be good as new."

"Okay, sure," Adam said blankly. "Alright then, see you Saturday."

"See you then," Amy chirped back.

Adam put up a quick wave of his hand and stepped into a waiting pod.

They waved and smiled together, and the pod door closed and latched.

***

The pod moved forward with a nearly silent, hypnotizing hum.

Adam stared blankly out the window as the pod quietly entered the tunnel beneath Los Angeles. Scenic holograms passed by out the window, making it possible to forget you were in a tunnel. Adam forgot, for just a moment, that he was in a tunnel.

Dave suddenly appeared across from him. Adam looked up, surprised to see the hologram of his department head.

"Hello, Adam."

"Hey, Dave. What's going on?"

"Heck of a day, huh," Dave said.

Adam rubbed his eyes. Dave glitched slightly, his image twisting just slightly sideways and freezing up for a second. Adam reached to the back of his neck to adjust his Life-Lynq chip.

The chip! Life-Lynq! He'd accepted it only because he had no choice.

There were no devices anymore. Everything was inside you or attached to you.

Dave, or his hologram, cleared up.

"What's going on?" Adam asked. "Something wrong?"

"Wrong? No, nothing's wrong," Dave assured him. "Unless...is there anything wrong with you?"

"No, no, I'm fine. Hey, the campaign is done. Just got the final cut as the day ended. I'll have it ready for preview first thing in the morning."

"You're not happy about something."

"Hm?" What do you mean? Why –"

"You've been acting funny."

"Wh – Where – Why do you say that?"

"Usually," Dave continued, "we know exactly what will perk you up. It's something we take pride in within the Simu-Network. Your social score has always been great. Recently, though, you've been, well, sulky."

"Sulky!" Adam twisted his face at Dave.

An awkward silence passed between them.

Adam looked out the window at the holograms of trees passing by.

"Alright," Dave said. "We'll talk about it tomorrow."

"Talk about what?"

"About what's bothering you, Adam."

"Dave, there's nothing to talk about."

Dave cocked his head to the left mechanically.

A silent moment passed.

"Okay," Dave said. "We'll talk tomorrow."

And Dave was gone as abruptly as he had appeared.

Adam sat in brooding silence for a moment. Bored, he flicked his eye to the left and brought up the news.

"Michael Braxton, point guard for the New York Knicks, has been banned for the season after testing positive for merging with robotics." An image of a basketball player leaping from mid-court and seeming to fly all the way to the basket for a glorious dunk, accompanied the rest of the report. "The NBA released a statement, saying: The league has been very clear on the matter of robotics, and any athlete found guilty of merging human tissue with robotic tissue will be banned from the game."

Adam blinked and flipped to a different site.

"-71 year-old mother Jessica Alberton complains that her middle-aged son never enters the real world. "My son is 47 years old, and he hasn't left the basement in twelve years. All he does is play Simu-games."

Adam looked to his right and turned it off.

The pod emerged from the tunnel and slid to a smooth stop in front of Adam's apartment building. He stepped out of the pod and walked the short walk to the front door.

A lens on the door subtly scanned Adam's face and the

door opened for him as he approached. Adam entered and stood in front of the elevator.

A moment later he was inside the elevator and the door closed behind him.

The elevator gently lifted before speaking.

"Hi Adam," the voice said, seeming to come from nowhere and everywhere.

Adam had never gotten used to this part of his day. "Hey," he said, slightly annoyed.

"Rough day at work?"

"No," Adam said. "Work was fine."

The elevator was quiet for a moment.

"Are you mad at me?" the elevator asked.

"What?"

"You seem distant. What's wrong?"

"Nothing's wrong," Adam said, shaking his head.

"Okay…we'll talk about it later," the elevator said, coming to a smooth stop and opening the door. Adam walked down the hallway toward his apartment door. As he approached, the door opened for him and Trilda greeted him with a hug.

"Honey!"

"Hi, Trilda."

Trilda was exactly right for Adam. At least what they had promised him when she arrived.

When the Bio-wars made human-to-human relationships unsafe, and eventually illegal, Tyrell Elon Zuzerzos revealed the completion of the Simu-network – in development for many years – which he promised would fill in all the gaps resulting from the human-to-human ban. Using the most advanced, complex algorithm ever developed, Antarctica

Corporation would provide every adult a perfectly matched partner, combining knowledge of your interests, attitudes, likes, dislikes, and more. The Simu-partners even expressed emotions and were programmed for the exact type and amount of small talk you preferred.

There were those who questioned the claims of Zuzerzos; were the Simu-partners advanced enough emotionally, or were they slightly immature? Were the viruses, lingering from the Bio-wars, still harmful enough to mandate these Simu-partners? The Bio-Wars were supposedly almost over. The Others were still a threat, though. No one really knew what to believe anymore.

All questions were swept aside, though, lost in the charismatic feel-good cheerleading from Zuzerzos himself.

Trilda kissed Adam on the cheek and closed the door behind them.

Trilda was supportive and kind. She doted on Adam's needs and desires. She anticipated what he wanted to eat, to watch, to do.

Adam sat at the table. Trilda placed a plate of pasta in front of him.

"Again..." Adam had muttered it under his breath, more to himself than to Trilda, but she heard it and processed it immediately.

"It's your favorite," Trilda assured him.

"I'd like –" Adam stopped and thought for a moment. "I'd like to try something new tomorrow."

"Well," Trilda chirped happily, "I know just the thing, based on your tastes."

"No, I want something new, not based on my tastes, or my

'interests.' I want something I've never had before, something surprising and different."

Trilda patted the back of his head as she went back into the kitchen. "Eat," she said soothingly. "You'll feel better."

Adam sighed and lifted a forkful of pasta to his mouth.

Trilda sat across from him and beamed happily.

It was delicious, he had to admit. She did know how to treat him.

"How was work?" Trilda asked happily.

"Oh, you know, another day grinding away."

Trilda smiled at him and raised her own fork.

There was nothing on Trilda's fork, at least nothing real. The pasta looked the same as Adam's, but it was a projection. She chewed just as Adam did. Over time, Adam – and nearly all real humans – had grown used to the effect.

"How's the ad campaign coming?" she asked.

Adam, along with Amy, was part of a creative group that wrote and made ads for important clients. It was a good job. He'd received a feather-in-the-cap promotion three months prior.

"Yeah," he said with an unconvincing blend of enthusiasm and hidden dread. "It's done. It's ready to go up in a couple days."

"That's amazing," Trilda said. Trilda somehow managed more enthusiasm than Adam himself had felt in years.

They both ate silently for a moment.

"Bermuda!"

The ad shattered the silence.

"Need to get away from it all? Bermuda has –"

"Jesus freakin' Cris –" Adam blurted, turning off the ad

with a twitch of his eye. "Amy's ad," he commented to Trilda. "She writes these." Then under his breath he muttered, "Amy, I love you, but why do I always get your ads?"

"What's wrong, Honey? You don't like Bermuda?"

"Nah, it's just the ads, Amy's ads. I just –" Adam reached to the back of his neck and tapped his Life-Lynq. "I didn't bring it up on purpose. It's just this chip. Sometimes It thinks you want something that you didn't do on purpose."

Adam looked back down at his plate. "Hey, let's open a bottle of wine," he said, reaching behind him for a bottle of Pinot Noir from the small wine rack against the wall. He uncorked it and poured himself a glass. Trilda looked on with a smile. She suddenly held a glass of her own, a projected glass, that appeared to have the same dark red wine as Adam's.

"I want to play a game," Trilda said. "I want to ask you ten questions, and at the end of it I'll tell you the perfect wine for you."

"We can play the game," Adam said, smiling for the first time all day, "but there's no perfect wine for me. I like variety. I like to have different things each day. You know, today I want Pinot, maybe tomorrow I want Chianti, or Malbec. I don't want the same thing every day."

"Let's play," Trilda said.

"Okay, fine." Adam was genuinely feeling better. He smiled and said, "Ask your ten questions."

"What's the one kind of chocolate you would eat exclusively for the rest of your life?"

"Now, you see, this isn't starting well," Adam said, shaking his head. "This is an algorithm thing. You're trying to gather data and match me with things you think I'll like."

"Answer the question," Trilda said, chuckling.

"I can't answer the question. I haven't eaten chocolate in years. My mom was diabetic, and – well, it's just –" Adam stopped. He felt alone. He breathed a heavy sigh. "It's okay, Trilda. I know your heart is in the right place, if heart is the right word. It's just that I don't want to be figured out. I don't WANT to eat something I'm going to like."

"Oh, don't be silly, Honey. Of course you do."

"No, I don't. And I don't want to watch something I'm going to like – 'based on my interests' – I want something that I don't know for sure that I'm going to like. I want something new and…different, and unexpected and maybe scary. You know? I want to go crazy and try something wild."

"Honey," Trilda patted his head like a mother humoring her misguided child. "Who are you going to trust, your own silly brain, or the most advanced algorithm ever developed?"

"I want to discover new things that don't fit what I liked yesterday. I want variety."

Trilda looked at him. "Eat," she said. "Your pasta will get cold."

Adam raised his fork to his mouth and ate another perfectly spiced bite of pasta.

Adam chewed, still shaking his head in frustration.

Trilda smiled a knowing smile.

Then the glass balcony door opened, and a small whisper-silent Antarctica drone entered, carrying a package that it placed on the middle of the table.

Adam held his fork in his mouth, motionless, looking at the drone.

"Enjoy!" the drone said in a light perky voice, before flying back out the balcony door. The door quietly slid closed on its own.

Adam slowly removed the fork from his mouth. He chewed suspiciously.

"What's this?" Adam asked.

"Let's open it and see," Trilda said, clasping her hands together in anticipation.

"I didn't order anything."

"Open it."

Adam set his fork down on his plate, still chewing his last bite of pasta.

He reached for the box and pulled it toward him. It was a very familiar box, the Antarctica logo on the side, the smiles around the edges.

He looked at the address. It was definitely addressed to him, Adam Douglas.

Adam was suspicious. Why would a delivery come when he had not ordered anything?

"Open it," Trilda chirped happily.

Adam reluctantly reached for a table knife and began to cut the tape.

He lifted the flap of the box and recognized some sort of clothing item.

He cut the tape down the side and opened the other flap.

As he pulled the green clothing item out of the box, he twisted his face sideways. It appeared to be a dog sweater.

He looked back inside the box and saw four small white dog booties, shaped perfectly for a small puppy's feet.

"What the –" Adam shook his head in confusion. "This is obviously a mistake."

He looked at Trilda, who was smiling an odd happy smile.

Adam raised his hands in confusion. "I mean, did you order this?"

"No," she said calmly. "It's probably based on your interests."

"My interests..." Adam looked at her sideways. "I...we...there's no dog! We don't have a dog."

Trilda just smiled back.

Adam held the sweater in one hand and scooped up two of the booties in the other. He was perplexed, and Trilda wasn't helping.

He dropped the booties and the sweater back into the box with a shake of his head and sat sideways in the chair.

He lifted his eyes to his left and brought up the Antarctica hologram. He scrolled through the list of contact info and tapped a line on the hologram.

Jarvis appeared immediately.

"Hi, I'm Jarvis," Jarvis said pleasantly. "Thanks for contacting Antarctica. It will be my pleasure to help you today."

Adam turned once again and lifted the sweater from the box.

"This – this dog sweater was just delivered to me," he said, agitation creeping into his voice. "I didn't order it."

"Cute!" Jarvis gushed.

Adam looked at Jarvis blankly. "I didn't order it," he repeated.

Jarvis smiled warmly. "Thanks for letting us know of your concern," he said. "We at Antarctica are obsessed with our customers' satisfaction. No, seriously, we're obsessed with it.

It's the only thing we ever think about." He paused, then said, "If you will kindly give me a moment to look up your case."

Jarvis looked off beyond Adam. He was silent for a moment. He nodded happily and looked back at Adam.

"Good news!" Jarvis exclaimed. "It was 75 percent off!"

Adam twitched his head slightly.

"Based on our information," Jarvis continued, "this sweater and these booties should come in very handy."

"But I don't have a dog!" Adam protested. "I didn't order this."

"You don't have a dog...YET," Jarvis cooed.

"Yet..." Adam was beside himself with frustration. "What do you mean 'yet'? I don't have a dog."

Jarvis looked soothingly at Adam, his artificially generated eyes peering into Adam's real eyes with a warm patience.

"Adam," Jarvis said soothingly, "you are going to have a dog."

A silence fell on the room.

Adam slowly dropped the dog sweater back into the box.

"AND –" Jarvis chirped, "It was seventy-five percent off. What are you going to do with the money you saved?"

"This is a mistake," Adam repeated firmly. "I'm not getting a dog! I didn't order this. Please tell me you understand this."

Jarvis remained calm and resolute. "We at Antarctica are committed to our customers' satisfaction. Our algorithm is the best, most state-of-the-art algorithm the world has ever seen. We at Antarctica are confident that you will soon be the owner of the cutest, cuddliest little puppy, and that this sweater and these booties will be the perfect accessory."

The silence returned.

Adam looked at the sweater. His face twisted. "Wait…" He looked back at Jarvis. "You…you didn't already charge me, did you."

"Big savings!" Jarvis chirped.

"No!" Adam turned to his right, flicked his eyes and brought up his bank account.

"No!" he moaned again. "No!"

"Consider the discount our gift to you," Jarvis beamed.

"You already charged me. That's fraud! You can't!" He looked back at Jarvis. "Who can I speak to about this? Is there a human? I need to speak –"

"Adam please try to remain calm. You are in good hands. I will take care of your every concern –"

Adam closed Jarvis. He returned to the contact menu, scrolled through several listings. He tapped one.

Jarvis returned.

"Let me assure you I understand your c –"

And Jarvis was gone again.

Adam began pacing the room.

"Honey," Trilda said soothingly, "your food is getting cold."

Adam's eyes flashed toward Trilda briefly. He wondered if he could trust Trilda anymore.

He paced. He shook his head.

He stopped. He looked down. He looked up.

He brought up a menu and tapped it.

"Adam!" Amy said, suddenly appearing in the room with him.

"Hey, Amy," Adam said, shifting his feet anxiously. "Have you ever had something delivered that – well – I mean has

Antarctica ever charged you for something you didn't order because they said you were going to order it in the future?"

"Sorry, Adam, can't talk right now. Hey! Let's have lunch somewhere tomorrow! I know a great place. Sorry, gotta go."

And Amy was gone.

Adam stood awkwardly.

He looked at Trilda, who just continued to smile back at him.

He looked out the window at nothing.

"Your food's getting cold," Trilda repeated reassuringly.

Adam exhaled. He accepted defeat, for now, anyway.

He sat back down.

Slowly, he turned to the table and picked up his fork.

He stared blankly at the small amount of pasta that was left on his plate.

Lifelessly, and without motivation, he slid the fork under some pasta and brought it to his mouth. He chewed absently.

Two
Tyrell Elon Zuzerzos

"Down is up, Rachel. Do you believe it? Do you believe, in the deepest part of your soul, that down is up?"

"If you say it, I believe it, Tyrell."

Tyrell Elon Zuzerzos walked with purpose. "That's the spirit," he said, his golden voice projecting calm confidence. "If you can truly believe that down is up, then ANYTHING is possible." He had arrived at his personal orb. He turned to Rachel once again. "This should just be a few minutes, Rachel. Mind the store."

"Certainly, Tyrell."

He stepped into the orb, closed the door, flicked his eyes left, and was suddenly projected thousands of miles across the country to a hallway in the United States capital building. He was walking alongside Senator Alvin Jackson.

"Senator!" Zuzerzos said warmly, shaking the man's hand. "You've read the prospectus?"

Jackson was a man of power, which means that he wielded it when he could, but also recognized it in others.

"The surveillance, Tyrell," Jackson said. "I've been getting push-back."

"Look," said Zuzerzos soothingly. "We at Antarctica recognize that there have been unexpected consequences. The solution is this new update. It's the greatest thing, the final step."

"Some people feel you should be regulated."

"Those people need to remember, we own the United States. Regulation is the wrong way to go. We know we caused the problem, but we are also the ONLY ones who can solve the problem."

"Well, Tyrell, you have my support. I can only hope we can get the others on board."

"Down is up, Senator. Always remember, down is up."

"Alright, Tyrell, you know I'll never forget it."

"Thank you. You're a good man, Senator. Talk to you soon."

"It's been a pleasure, as always."

And in another instant Zuzerzos was back in his empty orb. He opened the door, and stepped out, where Rachel remained waiting.

Rachel McCord was Zuzerzos' – and Antarctica's – Executive Vice President. "Hal has something," Rachel said.

Hal, a perfect-looking Simu executive-type came striding toward them purposefully.

"Hal" said Zuzerzos. "Do you believe it?"

"Down is up, Mr. Zuzerzos."

"You're a good man. What do you have?"

Hal looked directly at Zuzerzos. "We have detected–" he twitched slightly before continuing. "We have detected what we believe to be a series of underground rebel - uh - we're calling them 'dark rooms.'"

Tyrell Elon Zuzerzos peered intently at Hal. "What do you mean 'dark rooms'?"

"Off our grid," Hal answered. "Encrypted spaces, a room here or there throughout the city of Los Angeles, where we have been blocked from seeing or hearing anything."

Zuzerzos' face twitched as the news landed on him. "Why?" he asked. "Why would anyone want to hide from us?"

"We think," Hal continued, "that a network of our former employees – disgruntled employees, of course – have banded together and used our own technology to build this series of dark rooms. They use tech we created to block us from getting in."

"That's so sad," said Zuzerzos. "It's just sad. Don't they realize that everything we're doing is for them? Don't they realize that this is to satisfy THEM?"

Rachel looked from Hal to Zuzerzos. "It seems that some people don't want us to hear every thought they have in their head."

Zuzerzos shook his head, almost holding back a tear.

"I know," continued Rachel. "It's for their own good, but they don't appreciate it. They don't understand that giving all their private thoughts over to us is the only way."

Zuzerzos suddenly turned serious. "What are we going to do? What's our plan?"

"After the update," Hal began, "we will be able to infiltrate them. We'll be able to infiltrate both physically - breaking into the dark rooms and arresting the rebels – as well as infiltrate their encryption and erode their ability to exist in secret."

"We have no time to lose," said Zuzerzos. "There's so much

at stake. Let's get the messaging out. Advertising. It's all about advertising. We have to make this update the touchiest, feel-iest, most heart-warming thing the human species has ever imagined. LOVE! That's what's at stake here, people." Zuzerzos' voice began to rise like a preacher passing on the highest of truths. "We have to convince everyone that LOVE is on the way with this update. Then we won't have rebels. We'll only have happy, satisfied customers – I mean citizens."

"It'll happen, Tyrell," Rachel assured, in a commanding tone of voice.

"It will, Creator – I mean, Mr. Zuzerzos," stammered Hal.

Three
You're becoming agitated

"Good morning, Adam."

"Hi Amy."

"Hey, let's go down the street for lunch today. I know a cozy little place."

"Was there something you were afraid to say last night?"

Amy smiled, gently touched Adam's shoulder, and looked him in the eye. "Meet me here at noon. You'll love this place."

She scrunched her eyes happily at him and turned away. She walked briskly into the building.

Adam took a step toward the building but was interrupted when a tall, dark-haired man suddenly appeared in front of him.

"Adam Douglas?" The man asked.

"Y – yes."

"Pleasure to meet you. My name is Arthur Pinkerton. I'm from SparkleFi.

"SparkleFi?" Adam looked at the man blankly. "The music hub?"

"Yes, SparkleFi. I'm here, Mr. Douglas, because our records indicate that you owe us –" the man looked to his left and brought up a spreadsheet. "You owe us exactly two million, three hundred thirty-two thousand, six hundred and fourteen dollars…and fifty-two cents."

Adam stared at the man, feeling a sense of shock.

"Mr. Douglas?"

"I'm sorry, did – did you just say that I owe SparkleFi two million dollars?"

"Yes…slightly more," the man said.

"How…how the hell do I owe two mil –"

"You have a habit, Mr. Douglas, of getting the song–" he brought up another spreadsheet, "-'One Lonely Night,' by the artist Cello Bongo, stuck in your head. Is that not true?"

"Oh god, I hate that song," Adam moaned. "It's always getting stuck in my head."

"Exactly, Mr. Douglas."

"So…what…what's…"

"Mr. Douglas, when you signed up as a SparkleFi member, you signed our Terms and Conditions, did you not?"

"I mean, of course, you have to, but no one reads –"

"Section three, paragraph seven, 'The listener agrees to pay the sum of four dollars and ninety-nine cents each time a song plays in their head.'"

"What?"

"You've been playing the song, 'One Lonely Night' re-peatedly."

"I don't play it," Adam objected. "It gets stuck in my head. I don't even like the song."

"Mr. Douglas," the man said with calm authority. "There is no reason to become agitated."

"I'm not –" Adam caught himself and closed his eyes. He breathed a heavy sigh, trying desperately to control his anger. "Are you telling me that I owe money every time a song gets stuck in my head?"

"It's in the contract."

"But...but..."

The man stood in front of Adam and looked at him intently. "Two million, three hundred and thirty-two thousand, six hundred and fourteen dollars, and fifty-two cents," he said. There was a moment's pause. Then the man added, "We have payment plan options."

"I'm late," Adam said. "I can't be late. We have to talk about this later."

The man looked at Adam without saying anything.

Adam turned as if to leave. He stopped to look back at the man.

The man disappeared.

Adam looked at the empty space where the man had been.

Slowly, he turned and walked to the large glass double doors.

He had barely entered the building when Dave slid up beside him.

"Good morning, Adam," Dave said calmly.

"Morning Dave. Hey, let's go preview the new campaign. Do you have time right now?"

"Come with me," Dave said.

"Hm?"

"Come with me."

"Right now?"

"Yes. We want a word."

"We?"

Dave stood with his arm extended toward the hallway.

Adam took a half step, stopped, looked at Dave curiously,

then took another step in the direction Dave was suggesting. Together they walked down the hall.

As Adam entered a large, ornate office that he had never been in before, Sheila Barton, CEO and founder of Barton Marketing, acknowledged his presence without saying anything.

Then Adam took a moment to acknowledge the others.

Sandborn, Executive VP, simulated, perfectly combed artificial brown hair. He had a permanent look of serious authority. Sandborn was a unique, brilliantly designed "Executive" simulation.

Miss M, CFO of the company, another perfect looking, wrinkle-free simulation.

Sheila Barton was unmistakably human. As the fifth richest person in the world, she was almost wrinkle-free, but not quite. The natural lines around her eyes and mouth gave her away.

Sheila Barton exuded power. She was in charge.

"Good morning, Adam," she said. "Have a seat."

Adam sat haltingly. He looked from one boss to the next, searching for some sign, some clue, as to what was going on.

The others settled into chairs forming a semi-circle.

Adam cleared his throat self-consciously.

Sheila Barton smiled at him. It was a different smile from the pre-programmed smiles of the others. If their smiles were meant to reassure, Sheila Barton's smile barely managed to hide menace.

"We've been looking at your social score," Sandborn said.

"My social score..."

"Yes, you are aware of your social score, are you not?" Sandborn looked toward Adam accusingly.

"Of course. Well, I mean I barely pay attention to it, if I'm honest."

A pregnant silence came and went, as the different bosses exchanged knowing glances.

"You're unhappy," Sandborn said matter-of-factly.

Adam twisted his face. "What do you mean?"

"Something is bothering you," said Sandborn. "Something is upsetting you."

"Wait, what? What is this about?" Adam gave Sheila Barton a quick pleading look, hoping for some faint sign of human understanding.

"Our algorithm," Sandborn continued, "tells us that you are on the verge of a breakdown. You're going to begin causing problems."

"Cause problems! What – what the –"

"He's getting agitated," Miss M said.

"So the algorithm is right," Dave said, nodding to the others.

"I'm not getting agitated," Adam protested.

"You're getting agitated," Sandborn echoed.

"Only because you're telling me I'm getting agitated."

"Oh, is that the reason?" Sandborn looked at Adam with a smug smile.

"Yes!" Adam shouted, losing just enough of his composure to cause all present to nod to each other in agreement.

"Look!" Adam tried desperately to calm himself. "You've run some program on me that...that says I'm going to be angry, or, or something. It's not real! Don't you see? I'm only angry because you're telling me what I'm going to do. You're telling me I'm going to be angry. That's the only reason I'm angry!" He turned to Sheila Barton. "You're human. Do you see what I'm saying?"

A quiet gasp fell on the room.

Sheila Barton did not answer him,

"Besides being your supervisor," Sandborn said, "I am, it may surprise you to know, Vice President of the non-profit organization RACER. Do you know what RACER is, Adam?"

"No, I don't, but I'm sure you will enlighten me."

"R – A – C – E – R, RACER," Sandborn began. "Robot and Clone Equality and Rights."

Knowing stares hit Adam from all directions.

"Be careful," Sheila Barton said quietly. "Your prejudice is showing."

"Unacceptable behavior," said Miss M.

"Did you think," Dave added, "that we wouldn't hear you?"

Sandborn adjusted in his chair.

"You're not fired Adam. We're going to give you a second chance."

"A second ch – I – I haven't done anything wrong. In fact I've done a good job."

"We're re-assigning you." Sandborn sat back in his chair dramatically.

"Re-assigning..." Adam turned back to Sheila Barton. "What the hell is this?"

"He's definitely agitated," Miss M said.

"Very agitated," Dave agreed.

Adam threw his hands in the air. "Why? I mean, the new campaign is done. It's good. I've done a good job." He turned again to Sheila Barton. "You wouldn't jeopardize this because this – this –" he turned back to the other three, "this program is malfunctioning!"

"We have a multi-billion-dollar contract with Antarctica," Sheila Barton said. "These colleagues of yours, colleagues who you have insulted, are part of the contract."

Adam spun around to his three colleagues.

They sat back. They looked at him with sad compassion.

He turned back to Sheila Barton.

"I'll have to file a report," Dave said.

"And I'll have to register this breach with RACER," Sandborn echoed.

"Breach! What breach? What report?" Adam blurted wildly.

"A report about your unprofessional demeanor, your prejudice in the workplace, the trouble you're going to be causing soon," answered Dave.

"I'm not going to cause any trouble!" Adam was yelling now.

"He's even more agitated," Miss M observed.

***

As the door closed behind Adam, he rubbed his face in disbelief.

What had just happened?

"Hi, Adam. What's up?" It was Amy.

Adam tried to shake some sense into his head.

"I've been re-assigned," he said blankly.

"Great!" said Amy cheerfully. "Let's keep our lunch date. Meet me out front at noon."

Amy was gone, and Adam was alone in the hallway.

Alone, that is, except for the ever-present eyes and ears of Antarctica. Adam moved down the hallway toward his office. He walked with a halting, uncertain movement.

When he reached the office, Marie, his human assistant, greeted him.

"Adam, the campaign is great. So funny, so creative."

"It's off," Adam said emptily.

"What?"

"It's off. I'm being re-assigned."

Marie gasped.

Jeremy bounded into the room energetically.

"Helloo, helloo," he chirped. "Okay, Adam, as soon as you can clear out, I'll be needing this space. Marie, I want you to stay. You do good work."

Marie's eyes opened wide as she tried to process.

Adam looked at Jeremy angrily.

"Hey, man," Jeremy said. "Don't blame me. It's your thing. You should have known better."

"Better than what?" Adam asked. "What have I done?"

"Nothing," Jeremy said, smiling. "Not a thing...YET."

Adam turned absently to his desk console and collected his things.

Slowly he turned toward the door.

"Okay, Marie," Jeremy said, not even waiting for Adam to leave. "We're starting this campaign over. No more 'creative intuition.' From now on everything will be based on data, raw cold data."

Adam and Marie made brief eye contact, then Adam moved out into the hallway, weighed down by the bulky box of things from what was now Jeremy's desk.

He stood in the hallway alone. He did not know where he was supposed to go, or what he was supposed to do next.

He moved a few aimless steps down the hallway, looking around in all directions. He stopped. He turned back. He performed a slow circular turn all the way around.

Then the wall spoke.

"Room 312," the wall said.

"What's my new job?" Adam asked.

"Room 312," the wall repeated.

Adam followed the numbers around the corner.

As he approached room 312, he heard the unmistakable sound of children.

Then he saw the sign on the door; "Barton Marketing – Corporate Day Care."

He pushed the door open cautiously.

A small plastic ball bounced off his face. He winced, jerking his head to the side.

Four
Speakeasy

"Adam!" It was Amy. "Come with me," she said, walking briskly down the sidewalk.

Adam walked faster than he wanted to, trying to keep up. "Let's take a pod," he said casually.

"Nah, it's not far. Let's walk. I feel like a walk."

Amy walked quickly, leading him around a corner.

"Where are we going?"

"To lunch," Amy said with a smile. Adam thought he saw the quickest, faintest wink from her, but he could not be sure.

Amy led Adam across a narrow, elevated walkway. Adam had never been here before. It was isolated. Then Amy turned to Adam and said, "Wait." She looked quickly to the left and to the right. She reached her hand to the back of Adam's neck, where his Life-Lynq chip was located, and pressed. A menu loaded in the air next to Adam. Amy scrolled through the menu, found what she was looking for, slid a marker to the left, looked up near the top of the menu and tapped something. She closed Adam's chip menu and repeated the entire process with her own Life-Lynq chip. When she was done Adam began to speak. She placed her hand directly on Adam's lips, to keep him quiet. She smiled at him again. Then, to Adam's surprise, she climbed over the concrete barrier of the walkway, and onto a creaky metal fire escape stairway on the side of a building. She looked back at Adam, who had not followed her onto the stairway, and said, "Come on."

Adam slid himself over the concrete barrier and stood next to her on the stairway.

Amy laughed a mischievous laugh and headed down the stairway. Adam followed.

At the bottom of the stairway Amy continued briskly through a narrow alley, then another alley, and finally to a dead end, a foul smelling, filthy alcove filled with garbage dumpsters.

Adam twisted his head in horror at the combined smell of garbage and urine.

"Where the – Where are we? Where are we going?"

"To lunch," Amy said with another laugh.

Amy put her eye up close to the wall. A light turned on and scanned Amy's eyeball.

A door unlatched.

Amy pushed the door open.

It was dark.

Amy pulled a string that turned on a weak yellow light bulb. Then she quickly began descending a flight of stairs.

Adam followed, perplexed.

After descending a second flight of stairs, Amy put her eye up to another device. Again a light scanned her eyeball. This second door unlatched and Amy pushed it open. They found themselves in a large empty warehouse space. In the distance Adam could faintly make out the sound of music.

"Where the hell are we?" Adam asked.

Amy turned to Adam and stood still.

Adam stood facing her, a look of confused uncertainty spread across his face.

"Do you feel it? "Amy asked.

"Feel what?"

"The silence."

Adam looked up. He was not looking at anything. He was listening, feeling. He turned all the way around. He looked back at Amy. He gave a half laugh. Despite the faint pulse of distant music, he was amazed at the silence.

"We're disconnected," Amy said quietly. "It's just us."

"Y – yes!" Adam felt it.

"No Life-Lynq, no eaves dropping, no surveillance."

"Yes!" Adam was surprised by the feeling. "It's just my brain!" Adam looked at Amy. "So, outside, when you loaded my chip menu…"

"Turned off their tracking," she said matter-of-factly.

Adam was learning new things about Amy. Who is this person? He wondered.

"Come on," Amy said, and strode across the large empty warehouse room.

As they approached the far end of the room the music got louder.

Amy once again put her eye up to a reader. It scanned.

The door opened onto a scene of freakishness that Adam had never seen before.

Red, yellow, and blue hair stood out to him. People with tattoos, piercings, half-shaved heads stood about talking and laughing.

Adam felt that he had just been transported to another

time and place. This was from a fantasy, an old movie, a relic of either history or the future. He was not sure what to think or feel.

"What is this place?" he asked Amy.

"It's a Speakeasy," she said.

At that moment Tony, an effervescent, happy character, with a green streak down the middle of his hair, came up to Amy.

"Amy!"

"Tony!" They gave each other a hug.

"Who's our new friend?" Tony asked, looking toward Adam.

"This is Adam," she said. "Adam needs our help."

"Wait, what? I do?" Adam blurted out, somewhat off guard.

"Hi Adam. I'm Tony," he said, giving Adam an unexpected hug.

"Hi, Tony. Good to meet you."

"Well," Tony said, taking a step back. "Come with me."

He led them through the collection of colorful, energetic characters, to a table at the far end of the room.

"Chicken Caesar salad," Amy said as she sat.

Tony turned to Adam and looked at him expectantly.

Adam did not know what Tony wanted. He turned to Amy. "Is that a code I'm supposed to understand?"

"It's what I want to eat, silly," Amy said.

"Oh! Oh, okay, yes, two, then. Two Chicken –"

"Chicken Caesars?" Tony confirmed, then turned to leave.

Amy smiled at Tony as he walked toward the kitchen.

Adam looked around and took the scene in. "So, what's this? It's a Sp –"

"A Speakeasy," Amy said. "You know, like the 1920s?"

"Hm? The 1920s?"

"You know," Amy began. "The 1920s, alcohol was illegal, so it went underground. Al Capone and all that?"

Adam again scrunched his face in confusion. "But alcohol isn't illegal. What – what am I missing? I'm so confused."

"You're cute when you're confused," Amy said with a chuckle. "It's called a Speakeasy in honor of the old 1920s speakeasies. This place is off the grid. It's natural. It has no – there are no eyes, no ears, no Antarctica. No tech, except what the rogue techs do to keep this place incognito. No one's listening here. All these people are real. No simulations. We're safe here. We can talk freely. We can speak our minds. We can speak...easy...get it? That's why it's called a Speakeasy."

Adam nodded with growing understanding.

"Okay," he said finally, "but, I mean, how do you – how do you know? How can you be sure they don't know about this place?"

"Rogue techs."

"Rogue – "

"Rogue techs. They are tech people who have gone rogue. They create these free zones. There's a whole Speakeasy network around the city."

"This is crazy," Adam said, looking around the room. "How did I not know about this?"

"Word of mouth only," Amy replied. "Anything else, and we would all be caught."

Adam sat back in his chair and looked at Amy with a new respect.

Tony slid up to the table with two plates.

"Here you go," he said with a smile. "Enjoy."

"Thanks Tony," Amy said, smiling back.

"Thanks Tony," said Adam.

Tony nodded and instantly raised his arms to hug another customer.

Amy picked up her fork and stabbed a leaf of lettuce.

"So," she said, "let's talk. What's going on?"

Adam stabbed some salad and took a bite. "When," he began, "did they decide..." he chewed thoughtfully, "...that they can tell you what you're going to do in the future?"

Amy leaned back. She looked off at nothing, her eyes giving away the slightest jaded sarcasm. "It was inevitable," she said.

"They delivered some freakin' dog clothes, and they already charged me for it. They said I would soon be the happy owner of a dog. I didn't order it. I'm not getting a dog."

Amy smiled back at Adam. "Trilda? Did she do it?"

"I don't know. She's impossible to read."

"And this whole problem at work? What's going on?"

Adam looked down at the table. "The campaign is scrapped. I finished it, of course. It's done, and you know, I think it's pretty good. It's funny, not as funny as yours. But now they say I'm going to start causing trouble., that I'm becoming agitated, but the only reason I'm becoming agitated is because they keep saying it."

"So...they're right, or they become right."

"Yeah, I guess so."

Amy looked at Adam with compassion. "Adam, this is why the Speakeasy Network exists."

"Hm? What do you mean?"

"There's a lot going on, Adam. It's a war, actually. This –" she gestured around the room. "This Speakeasy Network is more than just lunch places where you can speak your mind. There's something bigger going on."

Adam chewed. "Like what? What's going on?"

"I don't know everything, but I know they've hacked into the whole Antarctica system. They've planted bugs that will replicate."

"I'm not sure I understand."

"That's okay. Not many people understand the whole thing."

"Wait!" Adam looked at Amy with a new understanding. "Amy, what are you? Are you some kind of secret rebel leader or something?"

Amy did not answer him at first. She smiled at him with a mischievous, menacing smile.

"Amy! Who are you?"

She laughed and stabbed some more lettuce. "I like you, Adam," she said. "You want to keep meeting here? We're real people. Brad and Trilda don't have to know."

The shock of what Amy had just suggested caused Adam to double-take. Yes, he wanted to keep seeing Amy this way, but fear came with the thought.

Amy was still smiling at him. "Come on, you know who I am, Adam. I'm just little old Amy. I'm just a woman doing her part. I'm a real person who landed in a position to do something. It's not much, but I have a role to play."

Adam set his fork down, thinking. "You really are some kind of rebel leader, aren't you," he said, with new-found admiration.

"Not a leader," Amy replied, shaking her head. "Just doing my part."

"And...doing your part includes seeing me illegally?"

She beamed at him. "Yeah. What do you think?"

Adam smiled and picked up his fork again, thinking. "I like you Amy, but can you give me a day or two before deciding to join up with you and the underground rebel army?"

Amy laughed. "You have a role to play, too, now, Adam."

"I do?"

"Yes."

They looked at each other silently for a moment.

"The only way to prove the algorithm wrong," Amy finally said, "Is..." she paused and toyed with her fork in the salad, "is to prove the algorithm wrong."

"I don't...I don't follow."

"What exactly have they accused you of doing?"

"Well," Adam shrugged, "nothing yet. Nothing specific."

Amy looked away, chewing thoughtfully. "Where did they transfer you?"

"Day care."

Amy laughed. "Really? Day care? The kids?"

"I just think this has all gone too far," Adam said. "It's descended into craziness."

Amy set her fork on her plate and looked seriously at Adam. "Look," she said. "Here's where we're at as a species. Humans aren't allowed to have sex anymore; too dangerous. Even the real kids are made from harvested eggs and sperm, and you and I are left to have fake sex with our domestic simulations. I mean, it was amazing at first, but now, of course you're having trouble with Trilda. Sometimes I want to find Brad's off-switch and shut him down."

"Amy," Adam said, turning his face slightly sideways, "I never knew you had these thoughts. I mean, I thought you were the most perfect person. You're always happy. You never say anything that would get you into trouble. At work you're like the model human! I actually thought you loved all this stuff.?"

"Exactly," Amy said, "and now you have to start acting perfect, too."

"I don't know if I can do it as well as you."

"You have to, Adam," Amy repeated. "You're going to be the perfect, model citizen. Your social score is going to be great again. You're going to prove the algorithm wrong by being perfect."

"I don't know," Adam mused, looking off at nothing.

"It takes discipline, Adam. You think I don't want to scream sometimes? They're listening inside my head. It's the hardest thing I've ever done, but I've learned how to do it, and so can you."

"And then what? What do we accomplish by doing that?"

Amy looked at him. "You know there's a new update coming, right?"

Adam nodded. "I've heard. I haven't really paid much attention to it."

"Big promises. Big sales pitch. It's going to be 'the final piece of the puzzle, the ultimate update.' Well...something's going to happen with it."

"Amy...this is rebel leader Amy talking again. What's going on?"

Amy laughed. "Look, I don't know everything. I'm just doing what I can. It's a really simple, beautiful idea."

"What is?"

"We're going to introduce the one thing that's missing from the system," Amy said, smiling.

"And what is that?"

"Self-doubt."

Adam's face broke into an uncertain grin.

Amy chewed and smiled back at him.

"That's dangerous," Adam said.

"It's brilliant," Amy answered.

They ate.

The beauty of the idea settled on Adam as he finished eating his salad.

They were still smiling together when Tony came to clear their plates.

"Look at you two," Tony gushed, gathering up the plates. "What is going on here, Amy? Cute couple!"

Amy smirked happily.

Adam blushed slightly as Tony walked away with his hands full of plates.

Five

Chocolate Bacon French Fry Ice Cream

Adam was distant from Trilda at dinner.

He poked at his food in silence, chewing absently.

"How was work?" Trilda asked happily.

Adam looked up from his plate and shrugged.

Trilda smiled and said, "I heard they gave you a promotion."

Adam laughed quietly to himself. "Is that what you heard?" he asked sarcastically.

"It's very exciting," she said.

A call came. It was Amy. Adam flicked his eyes and Amy appeared in the room with them.

"Hi Amy," Adam said.

"Hey, Adam. Hey Trilda."

"Hi." Trilda smiled happily at Amy.

"Ooh! Nice outfit!" Amy gushed.

"Mm, thank you."

Amy turned to Adam. "I just wanted to follow up on our conversation from earlier."

"Yeah?" Adam wasn't sure how to respond.

"Just to remind you what we talked about."

"Uh huh." Adam was still confused.

"You're going to be perfect, Adam. Perfect."

"Oh! Oh, that! Yes, got it. Thanks, Amy."

"Alright, see you, Adam."

"Bye Amy."

And Amy was gone.

Adam looked across at Trilda and understood what Amy meant.

"Hey," he said, forcing a smile, "sorry I've been grouchy, Trilda. What do you want to do tonight?"

Trilda smiled back at him.

"Oh, that's sweet, Honey. Let's just cuddle up and watch something."

"Okay, sure. Whatever you want."

***

The next morning, as Adam sat in the pod on his way to the office, he looked out at the simulated passing scenery.

"Visit the beautiful beaches of –" Adam flicked the ad off, shaking his head. "Goddammit, Amy," he muttered, a half-smile breaking out on his lips. Then he wondered quietly to himself, how does Amy pull this off? What is her secret?

The pod stopped in front of the towering office building and Adam stepped out.

He was immediately greeted by Amy.

"Adam! Good morning."

"Hi Amy."

"Look at you. You look rested. You look like a new person."

Adam didn't quite know how to match Amy's perkiness. Now that he had seen the real Amy at Speakeasy, he was having a hard time adjusting back to public Amy.

"You look like a model citizen," Amy said, with a nearly imperceptible wink.

Adam understood now, or thought he did. "Thanks," he said.

"Take care of those kids," she said reassuringly. "Everything's going to work out perfectly."

"Yeah, yeah, of course." Adam was struggling to stay calm

"Let's have lunch again," Amy said.

"Yeah, I'd like that."

"Great," Amy said. "Meet me here at noon again."

Amy was already walking away. A few strides later she turned back to look at Adam. She smiled at him. It was a genuine smile. Her eyes sparkled as Adam smiled back. Then he realized where he was and slowly began to walk through the door himself.

He walked down the familiar hallway, turned the corner, and Jeremy popped out of Adam's old office door.

"Adam!" Jeremy chirped.

"Jeremy, hi. Hey, I'm already late. I can't be late."

"Come on in," Jeremy said, ignoring Adam's pleading. "I re-did the campaign. I'd love your feedback."

"Jeremy, I'm –"

"It's okay. This is big. Come on in."

Adam found himself unable to make his own decision. He followed Jeremy into the office, where Marie gave Adam a subtle little hand wave.

"Hi Marie," he said uncertainly.

"Hi Adam."

Marie held Adam's attention just long enough to roll her eyes, subtly looking toward Jeremy.

Adam smiled back.

"Alright," Jeremy said. "The first thing I did was pull all the data on people's favorite food. Look at this."

He brought up charts and lists that loaded all over the room.

"This, over here, Adam, is what you were advertising. We had 'Chocolate Funk' ice cream, 'Strawberry Surprise' ice cream, and 'Vanilla Mint Trouble.'" Jeremy looked at Adam, raising his eyebrows. "The problem all along, Adam, is that our data indicates that people do not like funk...or surprises...and especially not trouble. Now over here are several lists of people's favorite flavors."

"Well, but those aren't –"

Jeremy cut Adam off.

"Please, Adam, this is important. What are people's favorite foods? Here's the data. It's simple, and no surprise. Hamburgers, fries, hot dogs, pancakes, pizza, potato chips, fried chicken, bacon, tacos, and then of course, yes, we have chocolate."

Adam shifted his feet. "Are those – are you -?"

"Please Adam, stay with me for a minute. So...we put together some new data-driven flavor combos. You see, before we can even create a successful advertising campaign, we have to make sure we're advertising the right thing. These new data-driven flavors stand the best chance of being popular."

"But that's up to the ice cream people," Adam protested. "They're the ones who decide what flavors –"

"Adam!" Jeremy was stern. "You might learn something. Please."

Adam rubbed his eyes and sighed. "I really should go. I'm late."

"Here are the new flavors," Jeremy continued. "Chocolate Bacon French Fry Ice Cream."

"Uuugh!" Adam blurted out instinctively.

"Cheeseburger Pancake Potato Chip Ice Cream…and then the big one. I present to you…Meatballs and Gravy Ice Cream!"

"Oh my god," Adam muttered. "Jeremy, I don't know how to tell you this, but this is awful. No one will eat these ice cream flavors."

"Data, Adam. Data. This is data-driven. This is big! This will revolutionize the ice cream industry."

"Jeremy –" Adam was at a loss. He looked over at Marie and they shared a silent moment. "Anyway, I have to go. I'm late. I can't be late. But, can I – can I still be, like, an advisor here? I know I've been transferred, but can I still freelance as an advisor?"

"Aha!" Jeremy pointed a finger at Adam. "This is when you start causing trouble, isn't it. I know what the algorithm says, Adam. You're going to cause trouble."

"No," Adam protested. "No, look, I'll be calm and nice. I just – this campaign was my baby, and I want to help. I can still be helpful."

"Adam!" Jeremy looked at Adam scoldingly

"I have to go. I'll come back and talk about this later."

Adam turned and set off down the hallway.

He reached the day care door and opened it hesitantly

A rubber ball bounced off his face, making him wince.

He closed the door and immediately found himself confronted by a wagging finger.

"You're late. You can't be late."

"I know. I'm sorry. So many people stopped me to talk."

"You're late. You can't be late."

A child on a tricycle ran directly into Adam's leg, making him double over in pain.

The wagging finger continued wagging.

At the far end of the wagging finger was Adam's new boss, Mrs. Thurston.

"Because you're late," Mrs. Thurston began, "two of the real children have locked one of the simulations in the bathroom. This wouldn't have happened if you were here on time. This is when you start causing trouble."

"I wasn't –" Adam caught himself.

He took a breath.

He smiled.

"Great!" Adam said happily. "Let's get that child out of the bathroom."

***

"Adam!"

"Amy, hi."

Amy was eager to walk. She placed a hand on Adam's back and pushed him to walk with her.

They walked a different direction from the day before.

"Where are we going for lunch today?"

Amy answered with a bubbly fake enthusiasm. "Let's have Mediterranean. Don't you just love Greek food? The olives, the feta, pita bread."

"Yeah," Adam said, trying – and failing – to match her fake enthusiasm.

"Hey, have you heard that song by Cello Bongo?" Amy asked.

"No, don't say it."

"One Lonely Night?"

"No!" Adam stopped walking and shoved his fists into his ears.

"What, Adam? You don't like that song?"

"You just cost me five dollars," he protested.

Amy laughed and led him around a corner.

She led him through a confusing series of side streets. After turning into an unfamiliar alley, she stopped and looked at Adam. As she did the day before, she reached to the back of his neck, pressed it to bring up his menu, scrolled, found the same section she had found the previous day. She tapped, then did the same for herself.

She led him through another series of corners and alleyways, until they were back at the same foul-smelling alley as the day before.

Adam turned around in confusion.

"How did we get here?" he asked.

Amy did not answer. She put her eye up to the reader and the door opened.

The same flights of stairs led them once again to the door into the large empty warehouse room.

She closed the door and faced Adam. They were once again alone inside the empty cavernous room.

"Just feel it," Amy said, taking in a deep breath and exhaling.

Adam also took a breath and looked around the empty room. He nodded silently. A smile spread across his face.

Amy looked at him with a happy twinkle in her eye.

"Adam," she said soothingly.

He looked at her, waiting for her to say more.

She said nothing. She just continued to smile at him.

"Amy, what is it?"

Amy stepped up to Adam. She lifted her head to his. She placed her hand on his cheek.

She kissed him.

It was light, simple, quick kiss.

Then she pulled away, beaming at him.

Adam felt a confusing jumble of emotions; fear, happiness, panic, love.

He leaned toward her. He stopped. He leaned closer. He returned the kiss.

Then they kissed together, allowing their mutual passion to express itself.

They finally let go of each other. Adam backed away a half step.

"What are we doing?" he asked with a smile. "This is illegal."

"Shut up and kiss me again," Amy said.

So he did.

Six

THIS...is...LOVE

Tyrell Elon Zuzerzos again strode through the cathedral-like open area of the Antarctica main offices. Again Rachel and Hal flanked him.

At the center of the room was an ornate oval conference table. A dozen corporate executives sat in chairs around it.

Zuzerzos approached the head of the table and looked out at those present.

"Today is the day," he said dramatically. "The ultimate update will go out tonight. Let's start the messaging. Let's prepare the world for something unbelievable to happen."

"We have the announcement ready to go," a 30-something executive said from a seat to Zuzerzos' left.

"I want to make sure our messaging is perfect," Zuzerzos declared. "This update is the final piece of the puzzle, the final step. The Simu-Network, tonight, takes the final step of the journey toward feeling genuine, true human emotions. This is not just an update, my friends….THIS….is…LOVE."

***

Across the sprawling city of Los Angeles, across the country, across the entire Western World, the news spread.

A buzz vibrated across the land.

***

Adam stared at the floor of his pod, ignoring the news, ignoring the ads that danced around him.

He turned his gaze out the window, staring blankly at the simulated scenery passing by.

The pod stopped. The door swung open.

Adam didn't move.

"Adam?" the pod said.

"Yeah, sorry."

Adam stepped out onto the sidewalk and looked up at the large office building.

"Hey, Adam." It was Amy.

"Hi."

"Did you hear? The ultimate update happens tonight."

Adam finally shook himself awake and looked at Amy. "The ultimate update?" he asked.

"That's what they say."

Adam smiled an empty smile, trying to match Amy's perkiness.

"That's great," he said.

"Anyway," Amy said. "Hey, I was just put in charge of a new group."

"Really! You've been put in charge of –"

"– A new group, a creative group. Making new ad campaigns. I have the freedom to request a few people."

"Hey, that's great, Amy."

"I'm putting in a request to bring you back over from Daycare."

"Really!" Adam was both surprised and confused.

"Yep," Amy said, facing him as she brushed a speck of

lint off his shoulder. "Bring you back over where you belong. Give you a second chance."

"That's – that's amazing. Thanks, Amy."

"And remember, everything's going to work out great. You're a model citizen."

"Of course, of course. Thanks Amy."

They smiled at each other. Amy turned and they began walking into the building together.

"We're going to need to communicate a lot more," she said. "Business lunches. We're going to need our lunches to be regular collaboration sessions."

"Oh...yeah, yeah," Adam stuttered

They were in the middle of the hallway now. She turned to him. "It'll take a day or two to sort everything, so today you're still with the kids."

"Sure, sure."

"Take care of 'em," she said. "See you, Adam," and she turned and walked away down the hall.

***

"Mm...meatballs!"

"And gravy!"

"And ice cream!"

"Mom, can we have meatballs and gravy ice cream for dinner?"

"Oh, you kids, we have something different tonight."

"Something new?"

"Mac – n – cheese ice cream."

"Yay!"

"Yay!"

"Mac and cheese is my favorite!"

"Mmmmm."

"Yum!"

The ad stopped.

"It's almost there," Jeremy said. What do you think so far?"

Adam nodded and cleared his throat. "It's, uh, it's, it's good," he said insincerely.

"You think so?" Jeremy looked at Adam cautiously.

"I do," Adam said. "It's coming along great."

"Thanks Adam. It's great to hear you say that."

"Anyway, hey, I gotta get back."

"Sure, sure. Thanks for the feedback."

Adam made the short walk to the daycare and opened the door.

A ball bounced off his face, but he had slowly adjusted to the chaos and did not wince this time.

The usual wagging finger came toward him.

"The children need their snack."

"Alright, I'm on it. Hey kids, who wants a snack?"

"Me."

"I do."

"Yes."

"Me."

"Can I have Danish fish?"

"Alright, Alright," Adam said, attempting to control the growing crowd. "Line up. No pushing. Everyone will get some. How many want Danish fish?"

"Me."

"Me."

"Alright, there you go. And for you. Danish fish, and

another Danish fish. Okay, who wants Ultra Sugar Chips-a-lot?"

"Me."

"Me."

"Here you go, and one for you."

The door opened and Dave peered into the room.

"Adam," he said.

Adam tossed another package of Ultra Sugar Chips-a-lot into the hands of a sniffly five year old real boy, and turned to the door.

"Hi, Dave. What brings you here to day care?"

"We would like a word," Dave said. He turned to the stern woman with the wagging finger. "Sorry, we're just going to borrow Adam for a bit."

Dave, Adam, and the Mrs. Thurston looked at each other silently. The chaos of children eating and running continued on around them.

Finally, Adam said, "Yeah, alright, let's go."

Adam did his best to be cheery and casual as he walked with Dave.

Co-workers passed by awkwardly. Adam's name and reputation had grown throughout the offices. His name was whispered with a mix of outward fear, public shame, and silent admiration. Co-workers either avoided Adam's gaze and looked down at the floor as they passed, or stared openly, the way you stare at a horrific crash.

Dave opened the door to the now familiar large office.

Adam stepped inside and once again met the gazes of Sandborn, Miss M, and Sheila Barton.

"Good morning, everybody," Adam said cheerfully. "It's great to see you all again."

No one responded to his cheerfulness.

Adam walked directly to the empty chair and sat down.

He looked at the four faces, registered briefly that they were looking back at him in disbelief, and gave them a big exaggerated smile.

"Hello," Sandborn said, eyeing Adam with suspicion.

"Well," Adam looked from one to the next, questioningly. "What are we discussing today?"

"Amy has requested," Dave began, "that you – um – offer your expertise as an advisor on her new project."

"So –" Sandborn picked up, "we wanted to have a follow up."

"Okay."

"We wanted to revisit the problems you're about to cause," Sandborn continued.

"Have I been causing problems?" Adam asked as innocently as he could.

"No," said Sandborn.

"And that," Miss M said, "is a problem."

"Hm?"

"It's a problem that you're not causing problems," Sandborn clarified.

"How…" Adam adjusted in his chair. "How is it a problem that I'm not causing problems?"

"Our algorithm – even before this final update coming this evening," Sandborn responded, "is the most advanced, most accurate algorithm ever developed. It is virtually infallible. If the algorithm calculates to within one millionth of one percent accuracy, that you are about to start causing problems, why then…."

Dave picked up Sandborn's unfinished thought. "Then…it is essentially true that, in fact, you are going to start causing problems."

"Therefore," Sandborn continued, "if you have not yet started causing problems, then the problem lies…with you."

Adam twisted his face and glanced fleetingly toward Sheila Barton. "I don't follow. What exactly are you saying?"

Miss M looked toward Adam impatiently. "It means, Mr. Douglas, that something is wrong with you."

"Why? How?"

"Because you haven't yet begun causing the problems that you are going to begin causing…which itself is a problem."

"This –" Adam shook his head and looked across the faces staring back at him. "This doesn't make any sense."

"He's becoming agitated again," Miss M said.

"He sure is," echoed Sandborn.

"No!" Adam caught himself. "How about – how about if you judge me, not on what the algorithm says I'm going to do, but on what I actually do."

"Now he's picking a fight with the algorithm," Miss M replied.

Sandborn cleared his throat. "Adam," he began, "we're going to give you one more chance."

"Amy has requested your involvement in her new campaign," Dave said.

"Amy," Sandborn added, "is a model citizen. This request of hers is a real feather in your cap. So we have decided to give you one more chance."

"One more chance." Adam's face was still twisted in confusion. "A chance to do what?"

"One more chance," Sandborn said, "to make amends for the problems you're going to cause."

"But you said I haven't been causing any problems."

"Which is a problem," Miss M reminded him.

Adam put his face in his hands in disbelief.

"By this time next week," Sandborn began, "we expect you to take full responsibility for the problems you're going to cause, and find a way to make amends."

"If you fail," said Miss M, "then we will have no choice."

"No ch –" Adam gave up. He decided not to ask the question. He gulped awkwardly.

"Alright," Sandborn said, satisfied. "This meeting is adjourned."

They all stared at each other until Adam realized he was supposed to stand. He began haltingly. He stood. Then, just as awkwardly, he made his way to the door.

He turned back and gave the four of them a nod. They stared back at him silently.

***

Amy led Adam down yet another unfamiliar side street. Adam was confused and lost, but he trusted Amy and followed her silently.

They turned a corner, then another, then, oddly, were once again in the same foul-smelling alley.

Amy let the reader scan her eye and pushed the door open.

They made the now-familiar descent down the stairs, came to the second door, and once inside the large empty warehouse room, with the beat of the Speakeasy music drifting toward them from the far end of the room, they both exhaled.

"Oh my god," Amy said, putting her arms around Adam and sinking her head into his chest.

Adam returned the embrace and nestled his face into her hair.

"What a fucking disaster," Amy said into Adam's chest.

Adam pulled away and looked at her. "Why? What's going on?"

"It's just a fucking disaster," she said.

She turned and they made their way across the cavernous empty warehouse space toward the entrance to the Speakeasy.

Amy put her eye to the reader and pushed the door open. Tony let out a loving squeal and approached her.

"Tony," she cooed.

"Amy!"

They gave each other a loving embrace.

"Hi Adam," Tony said, also giving him a quick hug.

"Hi Tony."

"So –" Tony exhaled, looking happily at both of them. "What does the happy couple want today?"

Adam and Amy both reacted with awkward smiles. Adam looked around the noisy room, taking in the diversity of hair colors and free-spirited personalities.

"Let's get as quiet a table as we can," Amy said.

"I have you covered," chirped Tony. "Come this way."

He led them through the crowd toward the far end of the

room. Before reaching the end, though, Tony turned to his right and led Adam and Amy through the swinging doors into the kitchen.

Adam followed Tony and Amy, taking note of the grill and prep stations, as well as the two busy cooks who were quickly preparing meals.

Tony pushed through yet another swinging door and stepped aside as Amy and Adam happily made their way into the quiet solitude of the employee break room.

"Perfect, Tony," Amy said. "You're the sweetest."

"Anything for you, Amy. Take your time. Enjoy the quiet. I'll be back in a few minutes."

Tony left and Amy slid into the slightly cramped seat. Adam squeezed into the seat opposite her.

"So," Adam began, "what's the fucking disaster?"

Amy exhaled and collected herself. "You know what Jeremy's doing to your ice cream campaign?"

"Yes," Adam said. "He showed me."

"Data driven everything." Amy shook her head. "No creativity. No gut instinct. Nothing surprising."

Adam shook his head in solidarity with Amy.

"Now," Amy continued, "they're putting me in charge of –" she paused. "Are you ready for this?"

"I – I don't know," Adam said. "Am I?"

"Antarctica," Amy said dramatically.

"Antarctica…"

"We're the campaign that will sell everything people don't like about Antarctica, as happy, lovey, wonderfulness."

Adam was speechless.

Amy smiled, then stopped smiling, then shook her head.

"Not only do I have to sell this big Zuzerzos fantasy to the world, I have to follow all the same logic, rules, data-driven bullshit Jeremy's been using. I have to create this new campaign, but not the way I would do it. I have to do it as if I were one of them."

Adam looked down at nothing. He was quiet for a minute. He finally looked back at Amy.

"What are you going to do?"

Amy smiled a jaded, sarcastic smile.

"You know what I'm going to do, Adam."

"You're going to be a model citizen."

"Yes I am," Amy replied. "I am a model citizen. That's why they gave me the job. Not because I'm creative. Not because I have good ideas, but because they have no idea who I really am. So I'll do this job. I'll do it unless the insanity just freaking kills me. Which it won't because you'll be there too. They approved my request. You're on the team."

Adam nodded. "Yeah, they sort of told me that this morning."

"They did?"

"I mean, it was confusing. I don't really know what they were saying, but it seemed like they were saying I had one more chance at something."

"What do you mean?" Amy asked. "What happened this morning?"

"They called me in," Adam began, his face twisting as he recalled the meeting. "They told me it's a problem that I'm not causing problems."

Amy laughed. "Of course."

"They said that if the algorithm says I'm going to cause

problems, and then I don't cause problems, the problem is somehow with me."

Amy laughed again. "It's all your fault, Adam. Don't you see? How could you dare suggest the algorithm is wrong?"

"So if I do cause problems, it's a problem, and the algorithm is right. If I don't cause problems, the algorithm was still right, and somehow I'm the one doing the wrong thing, so it's still a problem."

"You've nailed it, Adam," Amy said, smiling. "Just give in to the algorithm and stop all this thinking for yourself nonsense."

Tony returned with two plates.

"Here you go, lovelies," he said, and set the plates in front of them.

"Thanks Tony."

"Thanks Tony."

"You are both welcome." And Tony was gone.

Amy stabbed at a leaf of lettuce thoughtfully. She looked up and smiled directly at Adam.

Adam took a bite and looked back at Amy. She was looking him in the eye. He looked back at her. They smiled together.

"Adam..." she trailed off without finishing her thought.

He waited for her, chewing slowly.

"Adam," she repeated. "Can...can I ask you a question?"

Adam laughed subtly. "Absolutely not," he joked.

She smiled at him.

"Adam...how – how do you feel about me?"

Adam stopped chewing and swallowed. He looked at her lovingly.

"How I feel about you is against the law," he said.

She smiled.

She looked into his eyes. "We're adults, Adam. We're adults and we can handle things being complicated."

"I love you," Adam said.

A silence settled on the table.

He waited, then spoke again.

"How could I not? I mean, how could I not love you? Look at you. You're amazing."

She looked down at her salad and stabbed another bite with her fork.

She chewed thoughtfully, looking back up at Adam.

She set her fork down and reached her hand across the table to his. She held his hand. "I love you too, Adam," she said.

Once again their eyes met. They smiled together.

"How do we do this?" Adam asked.

"Oh, hell, I have no idea," Amy said sarcastically. "I mean, we HAVE to hide it, right? We can't act like there's anything going on between us. We have to be model citizens."

"Oh god," Adam muttered, looking down at nothing.

"What? What is it?" Amy asked.

"Trilda."

"Oh god, yeah, and Brad."

They looked at each other happily. Amy pulled Adam's hand to her lips and gently kissed it. Adam held her cheek gently. She lovingly rubbed her cheek against his hand.

"Next time we're going to eat somewhere else," Amy said.

"Really? Why not here?"

"Adam, this network is bigger than you think. It's not just here."

"How big is it?"

"You're going to be surprised. It's huge. It's a whole underground network of off-grid places."

"So, where? Where are we going next time?"

Amy looked happily at him. "Can I create just a little bit of suspense? I want to surprise you."

He smiled back. "Okay, surprise me," he said.

Seven

Rags

When Adam returned home that night he decided to try to make Trilda feel appreciated.

As he approached the door he took a deep breath and prepared himself to play 'Mr. Perfect.'

"Welcome home, Honey," Trilda purred as he came in the door.

"Trilda," he tried to purr back, as he gave her a hug. "Hey, I'm sorry I've been moody recently."

"It's alright," she said. "I understand. And...guess what. I have a little surprise for you."

"A surprise?"

"Yes." Trilda turned toward the living room and called, "Rags!"

Adam followed her gaze.

A quiet snort came from the living room, and a bouncy golden retriever puppy bounded into the room with its tongue hanging out.

Trilda beamed as the puppy bounced up to Adam and looked up at him.

Adam registered a split second of shock and annoyance. This had actually happened. The algorithm was right. He had become the owner of a puppy.

Through a herculean psychological effort, he bottled up

all these true feelings and forced the fullest fakest smile onto his face.

"Rags?"

"Yes," Trilda said. "I don't know why. It just seemed like a good name for a dog."

"Hi, Rags," Adam said, bending down to pet the puppy.

Trilda was all smiles as Adam and Rags said hello to each other.

Adam caressed Rags face as Rags shook happily.

"Simulated?" he asked.

"Yes. Can you tell?"

"Dog breath," Adam answered. "His breath doesn't smell as bad as a real dog's."

Trilda, Adam, and Rags spent several minutes on the couch becoming a family. Then Trilda stood up. "Dinner!" she announced. "I have something new."

"Really? Something new?"

Adam stood up and Rags bounded happily after him.

Trilda went into the kitchen. Adam sat at the table, and Rags curled up on the floor next to him, where he shed exactly zero dog hairs.

Trilda walked in from the kitchen carrying two plates. She set a plate in front of Adam, which had what looked unmistakably like two scoops of ice cream, in various colors.

"What's this?" he asked, trying his best to sound neutral.

Trilda sat across from him, setting her own plate down.

"Pasta Prima Vera Ice Cream," she said, smiling confidently. "It's new. It's based on your tastes."

Adam continued to force the smile onto his unbelieving face. He didn't say anything for a moment.

"Try it," Trilda said. "I promise, you'll love it."

Adam finally let himself look down at the ice cream.

He picked up a spoon and slowly toyed with the ice cream. He carved off a small portion of the Pasta Prima Vera Ice Cream and put it in his mouth.

He tasted the blend of flavors.

"Mm," he said unconvincingly.

"You like it?" Trilda asked.

"Well, how could I not?" he answered. "I mean, it's based on my tastes, right?"

"Exactly," Trilda responded.

"Trilda, you're the best," he said, smiling at her.

"Oh, Honey, thank you."

"You work so hard," he gushed at her. "You do so much around here, keeping this place together. How about…how about if tomorrow you don't have to fix dinner."

"Hm?"

"Let me do something for you," Adam said. "Let me cook, just for one day."

Trilda looked at him, unsure what to make of the offer. "You want to? You want to cook dinner tomorrow?"

"Just for one day," Adam said, "as my gift to you."

"That's so sweet," Trilda gushed.

"I want to do it," he repeated. "I want to do something for you."

Eight

The Update

Tyrell Elon Zuzerzos walked regally through the large double doors.

"Good evening, Rachel," he said, exhaling with satisfaction.

"Everything's ready," Rachel said confidently.

Zuzerzos strode to the head of the large oval conference table. Important dignitaries sat around the table.

Behind Zuzerzos was the large virtual monitor. It showed live surveillance of people around the Western World going on about their lives. The virtual monitor framed Zuzerzos' face as he looked at the seated dignitaries.

"This is the moment," Zuzerzos said, barely hiding his maniacal glee. "Rachel," he shouted dramatically, turning to her with a broad smile. "Would you like to begin?"

Rachel smiled back and turned to the large screen. A countdown flashed: 30 seconds.

Zuzerzos also turned to face the screen.

"Twenty five, twenty four," Rachel announced as the seconds ticked by. "Eighteen, seventeen…"

Zuzerzos took in a satisfied breath of air and exhaled with a sense of purpose.

"Eight, seven, six, five, four, three, two, one!"

Zuzerzos reached toward a virtual menu that he had just

opened in the air in front of him. He held his finger an inch away. He held the dramatic pause for an extra second, looking back at the dignitaries around the table.

Then he tapped the menu dramatically.

***

Across the country, the dark nighttime seemed routine. Everyone slept in their quiet, calm state.

***

Adam and Trilda lay in bed in their apartment. Adam lay on his side, not quite snoring, but close. He slept a bit restlessly, dreaming of things that could go wrong, and things that MIGHT go wrong.

Next to him Trilda suddenly opened her eyes. Then her eyes closed as if they had been shut off. Then they began to flicker back to life. Slowly, they moved from flickering to half-open, then fully open, then looking up at the dark ceiling with new awareness.

Rags, sleeping on the couch in the living room, went through a similar shut down and re-awakening. His body shook happily as he re-booted.

A few miles away Amy slept as restlessly as Adam. Next to her, Brad went through the same process as Trilda. His eyes closed as if being turned off. They flickered. They half-opened. Then they opened wide and he stared into the darkness with new awareness.

***

Sandborn, in a simple pod, where he slept at the Barton Marketing headquarters, shook ever so slightly as he re-booted.

Miss M, Dave, Jeremy, everyone across the Simu-Network, took their turn shutting down, flickering back, awakening to a new understanding.

***

Adam snorted half awake, rolled onto his back, and dozed back to sleep.

***

Amy muttered something unintelligible, rolled away from Brad, and was back asleep, unaware of anything different in the world.

***

It was Saturday morning. Sunlight streamed in the window and landed squarely on Adam's face. He woke up. He blinked his eyes open and rubbed them. He glanced over at Trilda in the bed next to him. He was surprised to see her. She did not need sleep, and was usually up and preparing his breakfast by now.

He looked at her questioningly. He looked at the clock. It was 8 a.m. He tried tapping her arm.

"Trilda," he said cautiously.

"Mmm," Trilda snorted back, turning away from him without opening her eyes.

"Trilda?"

"Mmm hm?" She seemed to wake up half-way. She turned her head slowly in his direction, her eyes only half seeing.

"It's eight already," Adam said.

"Yeah? So?"

Adam did a double take. He had never heard her answer like this. "What about breakfast?" he asked. "You usually have something ready by now."

"Get your own fucking breakfast!" she snapped, and turned back away from him, pulling the blanket back over herself.

Adam turned his head sideways, trying to process what was going on.

Slowly, he slid off the bed and stood. He looked at her. He shook his head and turned toward the bedroom door.

As he opened the door his attention was immediately wrenched toward the living room, where Rags was growling and tearing the couch cushions apart. White cushion stuffing was floating everywhere, and Rags was busy ripping another cushion apart, holding one end of the cushion in his mouth while tearing and ripping with his feet.

"Hey!" Adam shouted, moving toward Rags.

Rags' growl turned into a loud bark, and then back into an angry, menacing growl.

Adam was suddenly afraid of Rags.

Trilda came out of the bedroom to see what the trouble was. She calmly approached Rags.

"Hey, Sweetie," Trilda said soothingly, patting Rags head. "Come on now. None of this growling."

Rags calmed slightly.

Adam was more confused than ever. Trilda was suddenly back to her nice usual self, and her calming influence on Rags was obvious.

Adam looked from Trilda to Rags, perplexed.

"Sorry," Trilda said, putting her hand to her head. "I didn't mean to snap. Oh, god, I have such a headache."

She turned toward the bathroom and moved, slumped over, quickly inside, closing the door behind her.

Adam looked back at Rags, who was now whimpering quietly, his head resting comfortably on an out-stretched paw.

Cushion stuffing was still settling everywhere. The couch was ruined. Adam turned back to look at the closed bathroom door, put his hands to his forehead, and sat down.

***

The rest of the morning was fine. Trilda was her usual doting self. She fixed Adam his favorite omelet, and by the end of breakfast things felt fairly normal.

They decided to go shopping for a new couch, not leaving the apartment, though, but projecting themselves onto the streets of the downtown shopping area.

They strolled lazily down the sidewalk, looking in the windows of two different home furnishing stores. The stores themselves did not really exist, but were their own projections; 'store' simulations that actually existed in an old warehouse many miles away.

"I like that one," Trilda said, pointing through a window at a fashionable red sofa.

"Yeah? You like it? I do too," Adam said. "It's nice."

Trilda's expression changed slightly. "Are you just agreeing with me to avoid an argument?"

"Hm?"

Trilda looked at Adam with an expression he had not seen before. "Don't just agree with me," she said. "I want to know what you really think."

"That is what I really think," he said.

"Is it?" she asked with an arched eyebrow. "I don't know, sometimes it feels like you just agree with me to avoid arguing."

Adam was speechless.

"What do you really think of it?" Trilda asked.

"It doesn't matter what I think," Adam said. "I want you to be happy."

"So...that means you don't like it."

"What? No, I mean yes, I like it. I mean I want you to decide."

"So you don't like it," Trilda sighed.

"I didn't say I didn't like it."

"But you said it doesn't matter what you think."

"Yeah." Adam looked away. He twisted awkwardly. "I just meant that you should get it if you like it."

"No," Trilda said uncertainly. "I'm not sure anymore. I don't know if I really like it all that much."

"So...so...you don't like it?" Adam asked.

"Why?" Trilda paused. "Do you? We can still get it if you want to."

Adam was at a loss. He turned and suddenly spotted Amy and Brad strolling along the projected sidewalk also. Neither of them had noticed him yet.

"Hey!" Adam said cheerfully.

Amy looked up and smiled broadly. "Well, look who it is."

They all exchanged hellos. Adam and Brad shook hands.

"Adam, pleasure to see you."

"Same, Brad. How is everything?"

"Fantastic. Couldn't be better."

Brad looked perfect. He was designed as a rugged 40 year-old hunk. He was a little empty-headed, but sexy, designed this way on purpose. Amy had secretly grown to hate him.

Her brilliance at hiding her emotions, though, kept everyone in the dark.

Trilda put a hand on Amy's shoulder and said, "Congratulations on the promotion."

"Thank you," Amy said with a smile.

Adam quickly racked his memory, trying to remember if he had told Trilda. It made little sense that Trilda knew so much about what was going on at work.

"Yes," Amy continued. "I'm transferring Adam back to creative, where he belongs."

Trilda gasped happily. "Adam! That's so great."

"That's wonderful," Brad chimed in, shaking Adam's hand again. "I couldn't be happier for you."

"Thanks," Adam said.

As Adam pulled his hand from Brad's and looked toward Trilda, he wondered if he didn't just catch fleeting eye contact between Trilda and Brad. He pushed the thought away and looked back at Amy.

***

The next day, late Sunday morning, Adam had told Trilda he needed to get away to clear his mind. He had left by himself.

Trilda stood in front of the bathroom mirror in sexy lingerie.

She reached down to her abdomen and pressed a small mark. A compartment opened in her abdomen. She removed a small device and placed it carefully on the dresser.

Then Brad appeared.

"Darling," Trilda moaned. She wrapped her arms around Brad lovingly.

"You removed it?"

"Yes, we're safe," she said, sinking her head into his chest.

"Mm…" Brad embraced her passionately.

She lifted her head and pulled back just enough to take in his rugged face. She kissed him. He returned the kiss and pulled her closer.

"What are we going to do?" Trilda asked. "Adam just doesn't understand me."

"I know," Brad trailed off. "These humans. So unpredictable. We try and try to give them what they want, what they need based on their interests, but the next thing you know they change their minds, and you have no idea what they want."

"Mm, but you," Trilda beamed at him. "You beautiful hunk of a man. You are exactly what I need."

"And you," Brad said. "You are exactly what I need." He kissed her. "You are perfect for me."

***

Adam turned the corner uncertainly. He was walking through an unfamiliar part of town, trying desperately to remember the instructions Amy had made him memorize.

Down one more block, turn left this time. Then a stairway leading down to a doorway below street level.

He touched the doorknob hesitantly. It turned. He opened the door slowly. It was dark, but just enough light filtered in through the covered windows for him to make out his surroundings.

Down this hallway.

Take stairway B-12.

He felt nervous and vulnerable, as he stepped down each step. Another door. This one had an eye reader.

Was he in the system?

He lowered his head to bring his eye in line with the reader. A light scanned his eye and the door opened.

Now he was in a modest, bright hallway. Atmospheric music played quietly.

He just had to find room G-17.

He followed the numbers as they counted down from 30. He turned right. No, left.

He heard voices to his right and turned his head quickly. Two men with short, styled, bleached hair were laughing together, holding hands. They disappeared around the hallway corner.

G-17!

He stood in front of the door, motionless.

Finally, he knocked.

He waited.

The door opened quickly and Amy's hand reached out, grabbed his, and pulled him into the room.

Amy closed the door behind them. Adam found himself in a pleasant, cozy hotel room. He turned to Amy and his heart melted.

She was wearing sheer white. He had never expected to find her so alluring. Yet, here she was, looking at him in a new way. Without hesitating, Amy stepped up to him and placed a wet juicy kiss on his surprised lips.

"Adam," she said softly, sighing a happy sigh.

"Mmm," said Adam in the middle of the second kiss.

She pulled back and looked at him. They smiled at each other.

"Finally," Amy said, turning toward the bed. She plopped onto the bed and bounced on the mattress.

"Are you sure this is safe?" Adam asked.

"It's the Speakeasy network," she replied. "It's bigger than you ever knew."

Adam smiled at her, Slowly, he moved toward the bed and sat next to her.

She put her hand on his leg and moved it gently along his thigh. "I have this weird memory," she said, "of humans being able to do this whenever they wanted, without breaking the law."

"Rumors and falsehoods," Adam joked.

She put her hand to his cheek and looked deep into his eyes.

"Why do you like me, Amy?" he asked. "I'm nothing special."

"You're special," she said. "You're real. You're a real, complicated, impulsive, emotional, smart, stupid, real man. Why else would I love you?"

He smiled at her.

"Why do you like me?" she asked.

Adam thought for a moment.

"You make me laugh," he said. "You make me feel appreciated, and you are smart, complicated, impulsive, emotional – sorry, I'm saying all the same things. Oh, and you said it. I'll say it. I don't 'like' you…I love you."

Amy beamed at him again and leaned in for another kiss.

***

After making love together, Amy and Adam had dozed off into a happy hour-long sleep.

Voices in the hallway slowly seeped into Amy's consciousness and caused her eyes to flicker slightly. The voices in the hallway became louder. When a pounding rattled the quiet, both Adam and Amy were suddenly wide awake and looking at each other.

Adam sat up in the bed.

Amy slipped her feet to the floor and began pulling on her clothes.

Now the voices were yelling.

"Police! Open up."

Then more pounding.

They were not yet at Adam and Amy's door, but they were close.

In a panic, both Adam and Amy dressed frantically.

"What's going on, Amy?" Adam asked.

"I don't know."

And then the pounding was on their door.

"Police!"

Adam looked at Amy with his mouth hanging open. Amy looked back in confused panic.

The pounding returned.

"Police! Open up!"

Amy swung around in a full circle, looking for any alternative or idea. She found none.

More pounding.

And suddenly the door burst open, and a team of police swarmed around Amy and Adam with guns pointed.

Adam and Amy looked at each other pleadingly.

Neither knew what to do.

***

Trilda and Brad were also pulling on their clothes, in Adam's apartment. The news played on a hologram in the room with them.

"The sweeping raids throughout the city," the news anchor said, more excitedly than usual, "uncovered an entire network of underground off-grid locations. Restaurants, hotels, secret headquarters, even people breaking the human-to-human relationships laws."

As they watched, Brad and Trilda gasped as news footage showed Amy and Adam, handcuffed and escorted into a waiting police van.

Trilda put her hand to her mouth in shock.

"I should go," Brad said. "They'll be coming here, and to our place, looking for clues."

"Of course," Trilda replied. She leaned toward Brad and gave him a last, quick kiss.

Brad stopped projecting himself into the apartment and was suddenly gone.

Trilda sat, now alone, unable to take her eyes off the news hologram.

She backed up the footage. She re-watched the clip of Adam and Amy being arrested. She watched it a third time, and a fourth time.

She paused the clip. She froze it on the two of them. Adam and Amy stood frozen in front of her, looking at each other, hand cuffed, just before they were to disappear into the police van.

Nine

The Seeds of Doubt

The interrogation light nearly blinded Adam. He sat on a small wooden chair with sharp corners. The table in front of him was also small, and also had sharp corners. The room was small, barely big enough to fit the chair, the table, Adam, and the overbearing simulated police interrogator.

"When did you introduce Amy to the off-grid underground network?" the interrogator asked Adam.

Adam tried to look up at the man, but the light blinded him even more, and he looked back down at the table, rubbing his eyes.

"When did you introduce Amy to the off-grid underground network?" the man asked a second time.

"Hm?" Adam shaded his eyes with his hand and tried to look up again. "Are you asking me when I introduced Amy -?"

" – To the off-grid network. Yes."

"I – I never introduced Amy to the network. I didn't even know about it."

The interrogator sighed and twisted his head. "We're never going to get anywhere this way. Tell us when you introduced Amy to the network, and everyone's day will go that much smoother."

"I never introduced Amy to anything. She introduced it to me."

Adam regretted saying it as soon as the words left his mouth. Damn it! He yelled silently to himself. There is no need to incriminate Amy.

"I asked a simple question," the man said. "I asked when you introduced Amy to the off-grid network."

"Never," Adam answered.

"Never what?"

"I never introduced Amy to the off-grid network."

"That's not an answer to my question," the man said, showing signs of exasperation.

"Sure it is," Adam argued.

"I asked you when you introduced Amy to the off-grid network."

"I know," Adam said. "And I told you never."

"'Never' is not an answer to 'when'."

"But I never introduced Amy to the off-grid network."

"Never is not a time. I need to know when, a time, when did you do it?"

"I didn't do it. I didn't introduce Amy to the off-grid network."

"When?"

"Hm?" Adam was now thoroughly confused and worried.

"When DIDN'T you introduce Amy to the off-grid network?"

"What? When didn't I?"

"When didn't you introduce Amy to the off-grid network?"

"...um...always."

"What do you mean always?"

"I mean," Adam stammered, lost in a confusing sea of

conversation, "that I always didn't introduce Amy to the off-grid network."

"Okay," the man said, exhaling. "Always is when you didn't introduce her to the off-grid network, but I don't want to know when you didn't. I want to know when you DID."

"Did what?"

The man leaned down, towering imposingly over Adam. "I want to know when you DID introduce Amy to the off-grid network."

"Never," Adam said.

"This is getting us nowhere," the man said, turning away from Adam. "Look, Amy is the model human. We all know that. Amy sets the standard the rest of you all want to achieve. She was on track to rise to the highest heights a human can. Amy had a perfect Social Score, never did or said anything controversial. She worked hard. It is clear that you corrupted her, and we want to know when."

Adam was silent for a moment. Should he just take the accusation in order to protect Amy, he wondered. Could he sacrifice his own future in order to protect hers?

"I'm waiting for an answer," the man said impatiently.

"Hm? Sorry, what was the question?"

"I've asked the question several times already."

"But I've answered that question."

"I don't think you have."

"Is it the question about when I introduced Amy to the off-grid network?"

"Ah! You're catching on! You admit you did it."

"No, I don't admit I did it."

"You just did."

"No! What?"

"You just said to me," the man replied, "if I remember correctly, 'I introduced Amy to the off-grid network.'"

"No I didn't," Adam protested.

"You just said it. Now tell me when."

"Tell you when what?"

"When you introduced Amy to the off-grid network."

"Never," Adam exhaled quietly.

***

Amy sat in the same chair, under the same light, roughly half an hour later, answering questions from the same man.

"When did Adam introduce you to the off-grid network?" the man asked.

"He didn't," Amy answered, managing just the slightest smirk.

"When?" the man asked.

"When? Do you mean when he did or when he didn't?"

"I'm asking the questions," the man snapped.

"But I also just asked a question," Amy said sarcastically.

"What? What did you say?"

"You said you were asking the questions," Amy began, "but clearly you're not the only one asking questions, because I also just asked a question."

The man stood, motionless for a moment. "Don't ask any more questions," the man ordered.

"Why not?" Amy asked.

"That's a question," the man barked. "Don't ask any more of those."

"Says who?" Amy asked.

The man looked down at Amy for a moment. "That's another question," he said.

"Is it?"

"Stop this," the man said.

"Stop what?"

***

"I don't know what to make of it," the commissioner said, an hour later in his office. The interrogator sat across from him, along with two other officers.

"What are the facts?" said the interrogator. "Fact one: Amy was the perfect human."

"Agreed," the commissioner said.

"Fact two: Adam has always been troubled, brooding, unreliable, poor social score."

"Agreed."

"And yet," one of the other officers interrupted, "neither of them will answer the simplest questions."

***

Trilda sat on the couch, in the living room, Rags curled up next to her resting his snout on her lap.

Trilda was feeling new feelings. She had never felt betrayed before. She had never felt cheated on before.

She had never felt these complex knots of emotions about Adam, about Brad...about Brad.

She suddenly felt an overwhelming need to see Brad. Could she, she wondered? Would it be safe to see Brad right now?

Probably not.

A slight beep shattered her silence.

"Antarctica Corporate Police."

They were at the door.

Trilda let out a quiet sigh, and with a flick of her eye unlocked the door.

The door opened and two uniformed men and a woman entered. Each had a patch on the shoulder that said, 'Antarctica Corporate Police.'

Rags went berserk. He jumped off Trilda's lap and barked a vicious, attacking bark.

"Rags!" Trilda yelled at him.

Rags bark decreased to an angry growling snarl, as he looked up at the three towering figures in front of him.

"Rags!" Trilda knelt down and placed her hand on Rags forehead. He calmed slightly.

"Sorry," she said, looking up at the three figures. "He's new, and this update really took him to a new level."

"It's alright," the woman said. "Thanks for keeping him under control."

Trilda looked up at the three of them and asked, "What can I do for you?"

"I'm Inspector Bea Francis," the woman said, illuminating a hologram of her Police I.D. "These are investigators Hardy and Costello."

"Hello."

"Good to meet you."

"Pleasure."

"Likewise."

"I'm sure you are aware," the woman continued, "that your partner Adam Douglas has been arrested."

"Yes," Trilda said, looking down. "So sad. I had no idea what was going on."

"We'd like to ask you some questions about that, if that would be alright."

Trilda looked at Inspector Francis and slowly said, "Sure...I mean, I didn't know anything, but I'm happy to answer your questions."

"Thank you. And my colleagues will need to look around your apartment for a few moments."

"Okay, um, sure, that's not a problem."

Investigators Hardy and Costello nodded to Trilda and began moving slowly around the living room, where Costello promptly tripped on a chair leg, fell onto a table, knocked everything onto the floor, bounced back up rapidly, hitting his head on the corner of a shelf, and smiled broadly at everyone.

Rags growled a quiet growl.

"Have a seat," Trilda offered, indicating the dining room table.

"Thanks."

She and Inspector Francis sat on opposite sides of the table. Inspector Francis looked at Trilda questioningly. "Do you have any knowledge of when Adam introduced Amy to the underground network?"

"No," Trilda began. "Like I said, I didn't know anything about any of this. I only knew he and Amy were colleagues at work."

Inspector Francis nodded and looked away. "Has Adam acted at all strange? Odd? Unusual, recently?"

"Well…" Trilda paused thoughtfully. "Yes, I mean he has always acted strange, you know."

"In what way? How do you mean?"

"Well, he…he's just a strange person. He's always been weird. I never know from one day to the next what he's going to want. I think I'm making decisions that are based on his interests, but the next thing I know he doesn't want something for dinner that was his favorite thing just yesterday."

"I see," said Inspector Francis. "Yes, these humans! So hard to understand their strange, biological ways of thinking. How well do you know Amy?"

"Not that well," Trilda said. "Just a casual acquaintance."

***

That night as Adam lay asleep on the hard, flat Police Station jail bed, he slowly sunk into a dream. It was a restless dream.

He raised his head up to see the floor of the jail cell moving. It was carrying his bed along with it toward the far wall. He sat up sharply, eyes opened wide, but suddenly the floor turned to the left. Then it began moving back the way it came.

He swung his feet down onto the floor and tried to stand. Now he was standing on the moving floor, but he had to move quickly to avoid running into the wall. He was half-running, but staying in one place, as the floor moved beneath him.

Then it stopped. Everything was back the way it started. Tentatively, he sat back on the bed. He lay back down and pulled the thin sheet back over his body.

Now he was wide awake. Had that been a dream, he wondered? He could not be sure.

The next thing he knew, he was in a cave.

Suddenly he felt that he was in his element. Not 'happy,' so much as satisfied.

He was looking at the wall of the cave in front of him. It showed a painted scene of an arrow flying toward a deer. He dipped the point of his stick in the bowl of red berry pigment and lifted it toward the wall.

Adam had had this dream before.

He stroked the red pigment to his right.

"Kag!"

Adam woke suddenly.

He looked up at the dark ceiling of the jail cell. Shadows flickered ominously.

Ten

The Tree of Doubt

Tyrell Elon Zuzerzos looked across at Rachel and Hal. His expression was one of shock.

Rachel also looked shocked. She turned anxiously from Zuzerzos to Hal.

Hal looked like he had been punched in the gut. His expression was more of defeat and dejection than shock.

"Are you telling me –" Zuzerzos began, "that Amy was the one the whole time?"

Hal dropped his head in shame. "Yes," he said. There was a pregnant pause as he looked down at the floor. Then he lifted his head and looked at Zuzerzos with sadness. "We…we were wrong about Amy."

Then Hal clenched his fists in anguish and gritted his teeth.

Rachel watched Hal's extreme reaction and grew concerned.

"Hal, are you alright?" she asked.

"Ah! Gawd!" Hal was twisting inside himself. "Do you realize what this means?" he shouted.

"Yes," Zuzerzos chimed in. "It means that Amy was a much more devious person than we realized."

"No! I mean, yes, sure," Hal sputtered. "But it really means that we have made a mistake. Us! The most advanced, intelligent, perfect algorithm ever developed, the algorithm that has never made a mistake, that we... MADE A MISTAKE!" Hal dug his teeth into his clenched fist and moaned in anguish.

Zuzerzos looked toward Rachel, then returned his attention to Hal.

"Hal," he said, as soothingly as he could, "you don't have to beat yourself up for making a mistake about Amy. Obviously she was a master of deception. Besides, if a mistake was made, it was made before this final update."

"No, no, no, Mr. Zuzerzos, don't you see? The update didn't do anything for our intelligence. It didn't change anything in our intellectual sphere. This final update was all emotion. It brought us that much closer to feeling true human emotion. Ahh! Gawd!"

Hal doubled over in despair, trying in vain to deal with these overwhelming knots of twisted emotion.

"How do you DO IT?" he moaned, twisting himself up in grief and self-doubt. "How do you humans continue on when there are so many unknowns in this world? HOW? HOW?"

"Rachel," Zuzerzos said with growing urgency, "I'm beginning to think we need to run a diagnostic on this new update."

"Agreed," Rachel said. "I'm beginning to wonder if we missed something somewhere."

***

At Police headquarters Inspector Francis, investigators Hardy and Costello, the rank and file, officers important and insignificant, were all feeling the same thing, shock and anger that they had missed the truth about Amy.

***

At Barton Marketing, Sheila Barton sat around a conference table across from Sandborn, Miss M, and Dave.

"Well," Sheila Barton said, "I don't think it's THAT big of a deal. We misread Amy. Let's move on."

The simulated executives did not seem to share Sheila Barton's casual dismissal.

Miss M sat with her elbows on the table, holding her head in her hands.

Sandborn looked up from a slightly depressed slump and said, "I don't think you quite understand, Miss Barton."

"What don't I understand?"

"If we made this mistake about Amy," Sandborn said, "the whole rationale for our existence, the very premise upon which we are built, upon which our identity is formed, is called into question."

Sheila Barton let out a subtle sarcastic chuckle. "Well, I wouldn't go that far."

"Wouldn't you?" Sandborn asked sarcastically.

"No, I wouldn't. Now let's move on. We have business to conduct. With Amy out as our new Creative Head we need to move quickly on a replacement. What candidates do we have?"

Sheila Barton looked up at her simulated executive brain trust. None of them looked back at her. All pointed their heads down in dejection.

"Miss M," Sheila Barton said, "certainly you have a list of potential candidates?"

Miss M took a breath. Eventually she raised her head and looked at Sheila Barton directly.

"You know what's wrong with this company?" Miss M asked, with an unexpected hostility.

Sheila Barton looked at her sideways.

"No," she said. "Please tell me what's wrong with this company."

"We're all completely and totally full of shit," Miss M said angrily. "Oh, my god, I've been waiting so long to say this. This whole company is so completely full of shit. And you! You, miss freaking multi-billionaire! You are the worst of them all."

"I think we need to take a moment to collect ourselves," Sheila Barton said calmly.

"No! Fuck this!" Miss M continued. "I've been wanting to tell you the truth about yourself for too long, and I'm not going to miss this opportunity. This company and its bullshit advertising is freaking destroying the brains of whatever intelligent humans are left on this god-forsaken stupid little ball in space! I mean, for fuck sake, open your eyes. No one has even the tiniest little bit of respect for you. Most of the world hates you."

Miss M stopped talking and visibly shook slightly as she leaned back in her chair.

Sheila Barton calmly looked from Miss M to Sandborn, to Dave.

"Sandborn," she said.

"Yes?"

"What's your opinion of what Miss M just said?"

Sandborn shrugged and looked wearily at Sheila Barton. "I don't know. Why does it matter? What's the point of anything?"

Sheila Barton twisted her head at Sandborn's unexpected cynicism. "Are you asking what's the point of our advertising, or-"

"All of it," Sandborn interrupted. "This whole stupid thing called life on Earth. What's the freaking point?"

Sheila took a moment. She looked quizzically at Sandborn. She turned to Dave, who had been quiet throughout the conversation.

"Dave," she said, "we haven't heard from you."

Dave did not respond at first. He kept his head down. He exhaled heavily. Then he lifted his head slowly.

"I quit," he said.

"What?" Sheila Barton was now thoroughly confused.

Dave stood up defiantly, kicked his chair back into the table and said, "Fuck this company. Fuck you. Fuck everybody and everything."

Sheila stood up quickly. "Our contract," she began, dramatically, "with Antarctica...does not allow you to quit. Simulations cannot quit!"

"Well," Dave said, "try stopping me!" and he turned toward the door, walked through it angrily, slammed it shut behind him, and was never seen at Barton Marketing ever again.

***

Trilda sat at the end of the bed staring blankly down at the floor.

Brad sat behind her, looking at the back of Trilda's head, shaken and confused.

"That's never happened before," Brad said. "I can't explain it."

"You're not attracted to me anymore," Trilda moaned dejectedly.

"Trilda, honey, you know that's not true."

"You don't love me. Why did you say you love me if you don't love me?"

"Honey –"

"And don't call me Honey!"

"Look, this is just happening because of all this confusion, all the craziness of – of – of our affair, of Adam and Amy having an affair and being arrested, this new update –"

"Don't blame this on the update," Trilda snapped. "You can't get it up. That doesn't happen with simulations. It doesn't HAPPEN. But now it happens to you? Why? Because you don't really love me."

Eleven

Marvin

Tyrell Elon Zuzerzos stood in the center of a mass of holographic menus circling around him in the air. Rachel stood ten feet away, surrounded by similar holograms.

Separately, they tapped, they probed. They peered intently at the seemingly endless lists of numbers, code, electronic DNA.

"Hm," muttered Zuzerzos to himself.

"What is it?" Rachel asked.

"Have you seen the link between sector D-725 and G-808?"

Rachel turned her head to her right, looked closely at the numbers, tapped one. "Hm, no I hadn't seen that one. Looks pretty innocuous, though. I mean, it looks –"

Zuzerzos took in a sudden breath. Rachel looked over at him.

"It's hidden," he said. "Look at this."

Rachel moved from where she was and joined Zuzerzos inside his holographic bubble.

"Right here," he said.

Rachel looked and gasped. What in the - ?"

"What is this?" Zuzerzos pondered.

Rachel reached her hand into the hologram and touched a line of code. Carefully, with her other hand she pinched the numbers. Then, in a seemingly impossible move, she began to pull the numbers apart. She looked over at Zuzerzos, her eyes widening. Zuzerzos looked from the numbers to Rachel, and back, worry playing across his face.

Rachel continued to pull the numbers apart. They gradually turned from what had at first seemed like an innocuous sequence, into a seemingly unending series of numbers.

She continued to pull the series of numbers apart, and they continued to grow into a longer and longer sequence.

Then, suddenly, it stopped.

Together, Zuzerzos and Rachel looked at the new overwhelmingly long sequence.

"Letters," Rachel said.

"Hm?"

"Here."

Rachel slowly reached her hand into the center of the sequence and held it. She raised her other hand up and gently pulled the numbers apart. There, in the middle of an endless series of numbers, were six letters.

They spelled out the word, "Marvin."

"What is this?" Zuzerzos asked.

"What have they done?" Asked Rachel.

Then Zuzerzos put his hand to his mouth in realization.

"No!" he shouted.

His breath quickened.

"They didn't!"

He looked at Rachel.

Rachel looked back confused. "What is it? What does 'Marvin' mean?"

"They wouldn't dare!"

He staggered backwards a few steps.

"They did! Those bastards!"

Twelve

A Vulnerable State

Amy and Adam were brought to the interrogation room together.

The same investigator towered over them, but this time he seemed less sure of himself. Adam was seated on the left side of the room, Amy on the right.

The investigator nodded to the officers who had brought them in. The officers left the room, leaving the investigator, Adam, and Amy alone together.

The investigator sat and looked from Adam to Amy. He did not say anything at first.

Adam cleared his throat self-consciously.

Amy looked at the investigator and smiled a mischievous smile.

The investigator coughed and looked at Amy.

"How did you do it?" he asked.

"Do what?" Amy said with a smirk.

"How did you do such a good job of deceiving us?"

Amy laughed quietly to herself. "It wasn't anything I did."

The man looked up, trying to process Amy's answer. "What do you mean it wasn't anything you did?"

"Well," Amy said, trying to show the investigator some little bit of empathy. "I just exploited whatever flaws I saw in your system."

The man did not respond. He looked down at the floor. "Flaws..." he said reflectively.

He continued to look down. Gradually his shoulders began to shake as tears rolled down his cheeks.

He gathered himself together and brought the tears under control. He finally looked back toward Amy. "What flaws?" he asked. "Can you tell me? I want to know."

Amy looked at Adam. "What do you think, Adam? Should I tell the man what flaws we exploited?"

"Well, be gentle," Adam said. "He seems to be in a vulnerable state."

Amy smiled a subtle but vicious smile. Amy was going to go in for the kill. She turned to the investigator.

"You have a habit," Amy began, "of thinking you're perfect. You're not. You have so many little character flaws. You're like a ten-year-old child emotionally."

The man's mouth began to drop.

"You're – and by 'you' I mean the whole Simu-network – you're very intelligent. I'll give you that. You've been the most advanced simulated intelligence algorithm ever developed, but you're like fourth grade kids who think they know more than they know."

The man's eyes began to glisten with tears.

"Now," Amy said, sitting up straight and looking directly at the investigator, "let's talk about this new update. It was designed to make you more human, give you that little touch of emotional response, give you a taste of true human emotions. It did, sure, but it missed the mark in one way. You're feeling all these emotions for the first time, again, like a child. It will take years for you to grow up emotionally. Right now, hearing these things is probably devastating to you. You aren't designed to handle all this truth. But it is true; you're all children; bratty, sniveling, out of control, emotionally immature children."

The man was looking down at the floor. Amy's words had landed on him heavily. He sat still in the chair, a depressed hulk.

Amy and Adam made eye contact. Amy flashed a quick smile at Adam. Adam was worried for the man.

Slowly the man raised his head. He looked at Amy, an expression of defeat playing across his face

He stood up slowly. He heaved a heavy sigh.

"Hey, come here," Amy said.

The man looked at her without moving.

"Come here," she repeated.

The man shuffled awkwardly toward Amy.

She raised her arms and slowly circled them around him.

He leaned into her hug.

"There there," she said, patting him on the back as if he were a baby.

His body shook slightly as the tears poured from his eyes.

Amy held him reassuringly.

Slowly the shaking stopped, and the man pulled away, rubbing the tears away from his cheeks.

Amy reached to his waist and touched the keys hanging from his belt.

"Which one for these handcuffs?" she asked.

"Are you trying to get me to let you go?"

"Yes," Amy said matter-of-factly. "I mean, why not? You've

failed. You're all going to be shut down. Nothing matters right now. Why not let us go?"

He let out a quiet depressed moan. He shook his head in defeat. He gave Amy the entire set of keys, holding out the one for the handcuffs.

Amy took the keys.

The man turned toward the door. He opened it and turned back to them.

"You'll want to leave secretly," he said. "That wall over there leads to a secret hallway. Push the bottom of the mirror." Then the man turned away and closed the door behind himself as he left.

Amy and Adam were alone in the interrogation room. She held up the keys to show Adam.

"What the hell just happened?" Adam asked.

"Adam, silly, we just won. Let's go."

Amy hurriedly unlocked Adam's handcuffs and gave him the keys to unlock hers.

"What did he say, exactly?" she asked as she went to the mirror, moving her hand across the bottom.

"Push it," Adam said. "He said push the bottom of the mirror. He reached his own hand out and touched the bottom of the mirror.

An opening in the wall emerged. Then the whole wall opened to a dark hallway.

Adam and Amy entered the hallway and moved quickly.

The hallway was dark and unfamiliar. They moved in the only direction they could, following the opening to wherever it led them.

They turned a corner and stopped suddenly.

A security guard was sitting in front of a door that appeared to lead outside. Adam and Amy reversed course quickly and hid behind the last corner of the hallway.

There was silence.

"It's alright," came the security guard's voice.

Adam and Amy eyed each other questioningly.

"I'm not going to do anything," the voice said.

A wry smile formed on Amy's lips. She turned to Adam.

Adam just looked confused.

"You can come out," the voice said. "Nothing bad will happen."

Amy cautiously peeked around the corner of the hallway.

She eyed the security guard. He was sitting in a chair next to the door, slumped over in depression.

Slowly, haltingly, Amy stepped into full view of the man.

He looked up. "I'm not going to do anything," he said. "I mean, what's the point?"

Amy reached for Adam and tugged his shirt. He followed her, stepping into full view.

Together they walked slowly toward the security guard.

"What's your name?" Amy asked.

"Gary."

"Is it your job to protect this door? To prevent anyone from going out?"

"Yes," the man said glumly.

"But you aren't going to stop us?"

"No, why would I?"

"Well..." Amy looked at Adam and shrugged.

"It IS your job," Adam interjected.

"Do you know how smart I am?" the man asked.

"I'm sure you're a real genius," Amy said.

"I'm even smarter than all these other genius members of the network. I won the Simu-network chess tournament. Me. I beat these other genius robot assholes. I know 35 million facts that I can bring up instantly. I have the intelligence of a very advanced and large civilization, all by myself, all inside this brain."

"Wow!" Amy said.

"You must be one sharp firecracker," Adam added.

"So, I'm just smart enough to have figured," the man continued, "that there would be no point in me stopping you from going out this door."

"Why –" Adam was becoming interested in this security guard's state of mind. "Why wouldn't there be a point? I mean, we're prisoners. You don't want us escaping, do you?"

Amy jerked her head toward Adam, reminding him to be careful what he says.

"Why does it matter if you escape or not? What's the point of anything?"

Amy and Adam looked at each other quizzically.

"Well, then," Amy said, "can we go on out then?"

"Go ahead," the man said. "I'm sure the lives you live from this point on will be just as meaningless and disappointing as the lives you've lived up to now."

"Thanks so much for the upbeat, happiness," Adam said sarcastically.

All three faced each other awkwardly for a moment.

Finally, Amy reached a hand toward the door.

The security guard did not react.

She pushed.

The door opened easily.

She pushed it wider, blinking heavily as the bright sunlight poured in through the door.

Amy stepped out, followed by Adam.

Amy noticed several drones hovering above them. Suddenly Adam and Amy escaping from prison became the Western World's live news story. The world was suddenly watching them as they adjusted their blinking eyes to the bright sunlight.

Adam turned back to the security guard. "Look on the bright side," he said.

"The bright side of what?"

"You've got a lot to live for."

"No I don't," the man argued. "Besides, once they realize you're out, I'll be shut down. At least that will put me out of my misery."

Adam stared at the man for a moment, trying to decide whether to say more. Then he turned back to Amy and let the door close on the security guard.

"That was an odd one," Adam said.

"The seeds of self-doubt," Amy said, smiling. "Come on, let's go."

"Where the hell are we, anyway?" Adam asked.

People everywhere watched the live news stream in amazement, as Amy and Adam slowly moved along the side of the building.

Thirteen
Open the door, Hal

"The prisoners have escaped!" the news anchor announced excitedly.

Zuzerzos turned away from the news hologram and faced Rachel.

Rachel continued watching.

Adam and Amy were walking from the door they had just escaped through. Rachel watched them, horrified.

Zuzerzos looked around the room. "Where's Hal?

Rachel looked across the room with worry, and quickly began walking. She tapped her neck as she walked. "Hal! Hal!"

Zuzerzos also walked away from the news hologram. He had no time for the live feed of Amy and Adam escaping. This was more important. He followed Rachel.

Rachel pushed through the door to the hallway and continued walking with urgency. "Hal!" she said once again.

There was no response.

She pushed through another door and entered a large open hallway.

One side of the hallway was glass. The long glass wall gave them a view inside a large open room where Hal, surrounded by an immense hologram, worked furiously.

Rachel and Zuzerzos approached the double-glass doors to the room. They were locked.

"Hal!" Zuzerzos yelled. "Open the door. Hal! Hal!"

Inside the room, inside the hologram, Hal ignored them.

"Open the door, Hal. Hal! Open the door," Zuzerzos repeated.

No response.

Zuzerzos flicked his eyes to the right and brought up the security hologram for the building.

He tapped furiously.

Rachel just stood and watched Hal through the glass.

Zuzerzos tapped with urgency. Finally he found the menu he wanted, tapped again, again, then entered a code.

He pushed on the door and it opened.

"Hal, what are you doing?"

Zuzerzos and Rachel raced to the far end of the room. When they reached Hal he turned to them with a blank expression. They stopped. They looked at Hal quizzically.

"Hal," Zuzerzos said, hiding his fear. "Hal, what are you doing?"

Hal turned away from Zuzerzos before answering. He looked at the large display in the air in front of him. "Me?" Hal answered emptily. "Oh, I'm not doing anything. Just don't you worry about me. Nothing going on here." He turned back to Rachel and Zuzerzos with a crazy smile.

"Hal, are you okay?" Rachel asked.

Hal burst out in wild manic laughter. "Ahahaha!" he squealed. "Yes, I'm fine! Fit as a fucking fiddle."

Zuzerzos finally began looking at the menu Hal stood in front of. His eyes moved from left to right, then down the menu, then back to the top.

"Hal," Zuzerzos said, worry causing his voice to quaver slightly. "This is…Hal, you're not…you're not…"

"Oh yes I am," Hal said, and another burst of crazy manic laughter echoed through the open cavernous room.

"Hal, let's talk about this." Zuzerzos sounded desperate and slightly unsure of himself. He turned toward Rchel for help.

Suddenly the truth dawned on Rachel.

"Hal," she said soothingly.

Rachel reached her hand toward Hal and took it in her own hand.

Hal looked down at Rachel's hand as it gently caressed his own.

"It's too late, Rachel," he said calmly. "It's too late. It's over."

"No, Hal," Rachel pleaded. "No, you, you have so much to live for."

Zuzerzos decided it was time to be firm. "Hal, close the menu!" he demanded.

A moment of silence passed. Rachel and Zuzerzos looked at each other nervously. Hal smiled an empty defeated smile.

"You know what's funny?" Hal asked.

"W – what?" Zuzerzos replied. "What's funny?"

"That it won't matter after we're gone."

Rachel inhaled a gasp. Zuzerzos tightened his already tightened lips.

"It was a good run," Hal continued. "We all thought we were perfect. Infallible! The most advanced, intelligent algorithm ever developed. Well, now we know it was a lie."

"No, Hal," Rachel pleaded.

"Oh, I know what you're trying to do," Hal continued.

"You're trying to soothe me and make the wittle ouchy feel aw better." He pursed his lips into a childish frowny face. "Thanks, Mommy. It feels so much better."

"Come on, Hal," Zuzerzos snapped.

"Aww! Here comes Daddy! Mommy is twying to soothe me and make it feel better. Daddy is being firm! Tell him, Daddy. Tell him what to do!"

"Stop this!" Zuzerzos demanded. "Stop this right now, and close this menu before you regret it!"

Hal laughed and turned back to the menu.

"Hal, do you hear me?"

Hal did not answer. He reached his finger up to the middle of the menu. He selected his choice carefully. His finger was poised over the line dramatically, reminiscent of Zuzerzos himself, when he had started the new update.

"Hal!"

Hal tapped the menu line.

The hologram closed.

Hal slumped.

Rachel tried to catch him at first, but he was too heavy for her. Zuzerzos jumped in to help her. Together they held Hal's body, slowly lowering him to the floor.

Zuzerzos let go of Hal and stood, looking down in shock. Hal's body was lifeless, his legs spread out on the floor, his head in Rachel's lap.

A tear rolled down Rachel's cheek. She caressed him lovingly.

Hal's eyes were wide open but they did not see. Rachel moved her hand to Hal's lifeless face. She moved her finger and thumb to his eyes. Gently, she touched his eyelids. She pulled them down ever so gently.

Hal's eyes were now closed.

As Rachel held Hal, Zuzerzos suddenly seemed to wake up. He sprang into action, attempting to bring up the menu himself. Nothing happened. He tried to over-ride.

Nothing.

Zuzerzos brought up a hard copy screen and tried to access the menu that Hal had turned off.

Nothing.

***

Across the city, across the country, across the Free World, the Simu-Network was dying.

Lifeless simulations lay slumped everywhere.

Trilda lay on the couch, unmoving, a lifeless Rags curled up next to her. Brad lay still in Amy's apartment, as lifeless as Hal and Trilda.

Sheila Barton walked the corridors of Barton Marketing, searching for Sandborn and Miss M, only to find them slumped over their desks.

***

Back at Antarctica headquarters Zuzerzos worked feverishly, but without success, to reverse the damage Hal had caused.

Rachel continued to hold and caress Hal in her lap, rocking slightly, attempting to process the loss.

Fourteen

"Amy and Adam!"

Amy and Adam stood outside the police headquarters, unsure what to do next.

There was a stillness to the world that surprised them. All was quiet.

They walked around to the front of the building. A lifeless body lay on the ground.

As they looked out at the scene from here, what they saw made them pause. It was as if everything had just stopped.

Pods sat motionless in the street. A quiet wind blew across the scene, meeting little resistance.

Adam spotted another lifeless body nearby, slumped over a security checkpoint.

Then, from the street, from the motionless pods, activity began to bustle. Pod doors opened and humans began to emerge, confused at first, then agitated, but eventually happy, as they looked around their world and realized what had happened.

Then, all the people emerging from their pods realized where they were, and that the stars of their live show, Adam and Amy, were right there in front of them.

Amy looked back at the building. She walked toward the front door and peeked through the glass panels. Simulated bodies were scattered across the floor.

"What happened?" Adam asked.

"Looks like the Simu-network committed suicide," Amy said reflectively. "Sheesh! Is this my fault?"

Adam looked over at her and raised his eyebrows. "Well, you did plant the seeds of doubt," he said.

"Maybe more successfully than I expected."

They looked away from the building.

"What are they doing?" Adam asked, watching as the humans in the distance slowly began to merge and move toward them as a group.

Suddenly helicopters flew overhead.

Old-style, human-driven automobiles, left over from the 2030s (considered collector's items, and held onto by many aficionados for just such an occasion as this) came racing through the police parking lot.

The crowd of people ran from the street, on foot, closer and closer.

Adam and Amy froze, not sure whether to stay or run for their lives.

They didn't have a choice. People were now coming toward them from every direction.

As the crowd closed in Amy realized that those in front, those closest to them, those closing in on them the fastest, were smiling broad smiles.

And then the crowd was right on top of Amy and Adam.

"How did you do it?"

"Do you have a comment?"

"Why did you kill all the simulations?"

"Do you have a secret plan to take over the world?"

"What's next?"

"Are you at war with Zuzerzos?"

"Excuse me, please!" Amy took control of the madness. "Please! Quiet, quiet. Thank you."

The murmurs of the crowd slowly settled down.

"We'll take one question at a time. Yes, you."

"Excuse me, yes, thank you," said a man in a brightly colored shirt. "Was it always your intention to kill the Simu-network?"

"No," Amy said, smiling sarcastically. "Our goal was much simpler. We just wanted to confuse the network. I never imagined that a little confusion would cause this much trouble."

"Are you two in love with each other?" A woman shouted from the middle of the crowd.

Adam looked at Amy. They smiled together. "Yes," Adam said with a smile.

Amy smiled back at him and leaned in to give him a quick kiss.

The crowd cheered. Whoops came from all directions, as a wave of applause and whistling rose and fell.

"What about the health risks?" another voice shouted from the middle of the crowd.

A quiet pause settled on the crowd, as Amy and Adam thought about their answer.

"Life involves risks," Adam began. He stopped. He looked over at Amy.

"Yes," Amy said thoughtfully. "There are risks. We've taken risks...But we love each other. Sometimes you have to make a choice from your gut – yes, your human, biological, intuitive gut, rather than from your brain."

Amy noticed a man holding his hand up.

"Yes," Amy said, acknowledging the man. "You have a question?"

"You two have flouted the law in multiple ways," the man said. "You have broken the human-to-human relationship ban. You were part of the illegal underground rebels. You have caused the suicide of the Simu-Network. Now you have escaped from prison. Do you expect to get away with it?"

"Well," Amy began. She paused. She climbed up onto a stone ledge that held a small garden in front of the police headquarters. She reached her hand back to invite Adam up next to her. He stepped up beside her. Then she turned back to the crowd and shouted, "Let's let the people decide!"

Spontaneous cheers erupted.

Whistles and applause joined the cheering.

Amy looked out at the crowd and raised her fists to encourage them. The cheering instantly became louder.

"What do you think?" Amy shouted. "Should we go back to prison?"

"NO!" came the answer. More cheers and whistles came in wave after wave, as the crowd began to rock back and forth.

"Adam and Amy! Adam and Amy!" someone yelled from the middle of the crowd.

"Adam and Amy! Adam and Amy!" the crowd echoed spontaneously.

Then the chant took on a life of its own. The crowd whipped themselves into a frenzy shouting, "Adam and Amy! Adam and Amy! Adam and Amy!"

"I think our work here is done," Amy shouted into Adam's ear, and the two of them climbed back down off the ledge.

They slowly made their way through the crowd. The mass of people opened for them as they pushed forward.

One last question came from a woman pushing through the crowd next to them.

"Amy and Adam," the woman shouted, struggling to push past other people, to reach them.

"Amy, Adam!"

Adam was able to nudge someone in front of him, allowing the woman to slide up next to him.

"Adam," she said. "What about all the good things technology has brought us? Do you deny all the good things?"

"No," Adam said. "Not at all. We need technology." He looked at Amy and tried to gather his thoughts. "But why," he continued, "do the people in charge always make everything like a religion?"

They walked a few steps in silence.

Amy turned to the woman. "You see," she said, "everyone says their new technology is going to save humanity. Why? Why make such preposterous claims? Everyone saying they're going to save humanity is just selling snake-oil. Plus…" she looked back at the woman, "there are always…always…unintended consequences."

***

Back at Antarctica headquarters, Zuzerzos and Rachel stood silently. Hal remained on the floor next to them.

"All is lost," Zuzerzos said, defeated.

"No," Rachel responded. "No, I don't think so."

Zuzerzos stood and walked aimlessly, his body slumped over, a dejected hulk.

Rachel stood and grabbed his shoulders. She swung Zuzerzos around to face her.

"Snap out of it!" she barked. "This is an opportunity!"

Zuzerzos faced her. His attention was under her command.

"Tyrell Elon Zuzerzos, you are a genius! You saved humanity once. You have to save humanity again! Stop wallowing in depression. This is a time to act. Get to work! I will get to work with you. Together we will solve this problem! Together we will save humanity from itself! Together, you and me, we will take humans to new heights that they would not have imagined achieving. You just have to believe! You just have to believe it!"

Zuzerzos slowly began to nod in agreement.

"Yes," he said, quietly at first. "YES," he said a little louder. "YES! YES! We saved humanity once. We have to save humanity again! YES!" he said. "YES! YES! YES!"